Kidnapped!

Deciding that some breakfast might help the empty feeling inside her, Elizabeth poured some cereal and milk into a bowl. Before she started eating, she was startled by the sound of someone on the back porch. It was so early—not even seven—that Elizabeth couldn't imagine who would want to visit this early in the morning.

Suddenly thinking it might be Patrick, she ran to the door, but no one was there. She looked around carefully before noticing the tip of a white envelope stuck in the outer doorframe.

Curious, she pulled it out and examined it. There was no name on it so Elizabeth tore it open. Inside was a piece of paper with crude writing on it:

WE HAVE PATRICK. STOP LOOKING FOR HIM. IF YOU DON'T IT COULD BE VERY BAD . . .

Bantam Skylark Books in the SWEET VALLEY TWINS series
Ask your bookseller for the books you have missed.

Sweet Valley Twins Super Editions

SWEET VALLEY TWINS

Taking Charge

Written by
Jamie Suzanne

Created by
FRANCINE PASCAL

A BANTAM SKYLARK BOOK®
TORONTO · NEW YORK · LONDON · SYDNEY · AUCKLAND

To
Matthew Julian Weiss

RL 4, 008–012

TAKING CHARGE
A Bantam Skylark Book / February 1989

*Sweet Valley High ® and Sweet Valley Twins are trademarks of
Francine Pascal.*

Conceived by Francine Pascal

*Produced by Daniel Weiss Associates, Inc.,
27 West 20th Street, New York, NY 10011*

Cover by James Mathewuse

ISBN 0-553-15669-1

Published simultaneously in the United States and Canada

PRINTED IN THE UNITED STATES OF AMERICA

O   0 9 8 7 6 5 4 3 2 1

One

◇

"I'm starving!" Jessica Wakefield exclaimed as she slammed her school books down on the kitchen counter. "I hope there's something good to eat." She opened the refrigerator door with a flourish.

Her twin sister, Elizabeth, peered over Jessica's shoulder. "There's leftover roast beef from last night. We could make sandwiches." She turned and looked at their friend Patrick Morris who was still standing by the screen door. "Do you want a sandwich, Patrick?"

Patrick shifted his weight and pushed his brown hair out of his eyes. "No, thanks, Elizabeth. I should be getting home."

"Oh, stay, Pat," Jessica said, balancing the roast beef, mustard, and a head of lettuce in her hands. She kicked the refrigerator door shut with her foot. "We hardly ever get to see you."

Patrick lived in an old-fashioned shingle house

just a few blocks away from the Wakefields, but Jessica didn't like to go over to his house. She thought Patrick's parents were far too strict. That, however, didn't stop her from liking Patrick. They had known each other since kindergarten and she knew that he was one of the nicest, friendliest, and cutest boys in Sweet Valley Middle School.

"Come on, Pat," Elizabeth wheedled. "You can stay a few minutes, can't you?"

A worried look passed over Patrick's face. Then he smiled. "I just remembered, my mom had to take my little brothers to buy shoes so she won't be home for a while. I guess I can stay for a minute." He walked over to the kitchen counter where Jessica was looking at the assorted sandwich ingredients.

"Liz, could you make the sandwiches?" Jessica asked.

Elizabeth sighed. Jessica was always finding an excuse for her to do the messy stuff. "Can't you, Jess?"

"But you make them so neatly."

Elizabeth had to admit this was true. Jessica tended to be sloppy. When she made sandwiches, they always fell apart when you picked them up. "All right," Elizabeth said. She couldn't help smiling as she unwrapped the roast beef and laid out six slices of bread.

Sometimes Elizabeth found it hard to believe that she and Jessica were identical twins. They both had long, silky blond hair, blue-green eyes, and dimples that showed when they smiled. But they were complete opposites in personality. Elizabeth was a conscientious student who loved to read and write. She was proud to be the editor of the sixth-grade student newspaper, *The Sweet Valley Sixers*, and she liked to do things to perfection.

Jessica was spontaneous and carefree. She spent most of her time with members of the Unicorn Club, an exclusive group of popular girls who liked to shop and talk about boys. And, as far as she was concerned, no party ever started until she got there. But even with their differences, they were still very close. And right now they were both thinking how unhappy Patrick seemed to be with his situation at home. Lately, all he talked about was how strict his parents were.

"I can't believe your mother lets you eat whatever you want," Patrick said.

"Doesn't your mother let you have a snack after school?" Jessica asked.

Patrick looked embarrassed. "She used to let me, but now she says three meals are enough."

"Maybe she doesn't want you to get fat," Jessica said. She and Elizabeth looked at Patrick and all three of them burst out laughing. Patrick was as skinny as a broom handle. There wasn't much chance of him ever getting fat.

"I don't know what's wrong with my parents, lately," he said. "They've been strict, but now they're really overdoing it."

"What do you mean?" Jessica asked.

"Well, it seems like they don't trust me anymore. They've cut my allowance in half, I'm not allowed to talk on the telephone after six o'clock, and I can't have more than one friend over at a time."

"You're kidding," Jessica said, appalled by the gloomy situation. *Those things would be considered punishments in our house,* she thought to herself.

"They even make me do three hours of homework every night."

"But sometimes we don't even get three hours of homework," Elizabeth pointed out.

"Then I have to do extra reading, so I can stay ahead."

Elizabeth cut the sandwiches in half. "Doing extra reading doesn't sound so bad."

Jessica and Patrick looked at her with such horror that Elizabeth had to laugh. "Well, it's not so bad if you can choose what you want to read," she said in self-defense.

"Like Amanda Howard mysteries," Jessica said, naming Elizabeth's favorite author.

Patrick shook his head. "But I don't have a choice. For me, it's either science or math. My worst subjects."

"That reminds me, we're picking partners for our science projects tomorrow," Jessica interrupted.

Elizabeth handed Jessica and Patrick each a sandwich and they all sat down at the kitchen table. "What kind of science project?" she asked. She was in a different class than Jessica and Patrick.

"We can do anything we want," Patrick answered. "But the best project will go on to be part of the district science fair."

"Lila and I are going to do ours together," Jessica said. Lila Fowler, one of the most popular girls in the sixth grade and a fellow Unicorn, was one of Jessica's best friends. "It's going to be great—but easy."

Elizabeth laughed. "That sounds like a terrific combination—if you can manage it."

"We will," Jessica said huffily. She didn't know what it would be yet, but Lila always had a way of making projects look harder than they really were.

"What are you going to do yours on, Patrick?" Elizabeth asked.

"I don't know." His worried look was back. "Even with the extra reading, I'm not so hot in science."

"Well, I'm sure you'll think of something," Elizabeth said. "Anyone want something to drink?"

"I'd love something to drink," said a voice from the doorway. It was Steven Wakefield, the twins' fourteen-year-old brother. Sometimes, Steven could be a fantastic big brother, but most times he was the world's biggest pest. Spying the roast beef sandwiches, he pulled up a chair to the kitchen table and helped himself to Elizabeth's untouched half.

"Hey," she protested. "Make your own."

"Why should I?" he asked, his mouth full of food. "This one's already made."

"Steven, you're gross," Jessica said with a grimace. Actually, several of her friends thought he was pretty cute.

"How about those drinks you were offering?" Steven swallowed his bite of sandwich. "I'll take some lemonade."

Elizabeth shook her head. "You pour the drinks. That's the least you can do after stealing my sandwich."

Steven shrugged. "I'm too thirsty to argue. Come on, Pat. Help me."

Patrick got up and took the pitcher of lemonade from the refrigerator while Steven got out the glasses.

"There you go, girls. Service with a smile." Steven put down the glasses and made an ape face by turning his lips inside out.

"Steven!" Jessica yelled.

Steven laughed as he poured himself some lemonade. He picked up the glass and the half-eaten sandwich he'd been working on. "I'm going to watch the end of the baseball game. Want to come, Pat?"

"Thanks." Pat hesitated a moment. "But I've got to be going soon."

"Maybe next time," Steven said agreeably. "Let me know when supper's on," he called to the twins over his shoulder.

"Food," Elizabeth muttered. "That's all he thinks about."

"And sports," Jessica added.

They smiled at each other. "And girls," they said in unison.

At the sound of the telephone ringing, Jessica leapt up, certain the call was for her.

"I think it's your mother," she said with disappointment, handing the phone to Patrick. Patrick's face fell as he took the receiver. "Sorry, Mom. OK, I'll be right there."

"Your mom came home early," Jessica guessed when Patrick hung up.

"She sure did," Patrick said, looking around for his backpack. "I'd better get going or there's going to be trouble." He grabbed his pack and flew out the door.

"I really feel sorry for him," Jessica said as she refilled her glass of lemonade.

"Do you think things at his house are really as awful as he says?" Elizabeth wondered.

"Why would he make those things up?" Jessica said. "Besides, you didn't hear how mean his mother sounded over the phone."

The screen door slammed and Mrs. Wakefield came in carrying a bag of groceries. With her fair hair and blue eyes, she looked like an older version of the twins. "Whose mother was mean? Not yours, I hope."

Elizabeth shook her head. "No way."

"Mom, what do you think of parents who make you do three hours of homework and don't allow any phone calls after six?" Jessica demanded.

Mrs. Wakefield sat down, slipped out of her high heels, and rubbed her feet. She worked part-time as an interior decorator and was often tired at the end of the day. "I'm not going to judge the way other people run their families, honey. It's hard enough for parents to take care of their own kids." Mrs. Wakefield yawned. "I'd like to lie down for a while before I start supper. Will you girls put the groceries away?"

Elizabeth and Jessica nodded.

Mrs. Wakefield thanked her daughters and went upstairs. As soon as she was out of hearing distance, Elizabeth said, "Jess, we shouldn't be gossiping about what goes on in the Morris house."

"What's the big deal?" Jessica grumbled. "If the Morrises are being that terrible, I think other people should know about it." She got up and halfheartedly put away some eggs and a carton of milk.

Elizabeth got up to help Jessica. "Well, *we* shouldn't be the ones to go telling everyone," she replied.

"All I know is that if even half of what Patrick says is true, I couldn't last one day in his house." With that, Jessica started out of the kitchen.

"Hey, where do you think you're going?" Elizabeth asked, removing some cans of soup from the bag.

"I have to get started on my homework," Jessica said, standing in the kitchen doorway.

"But we're not done putting away the groceries."

"Can't you help me out this once, Lizzie? I just remembered, I have a book report due tomorrow and I haven't even started it yet."

"Jessica . . ."

Before she could argue any further, Jessica was halfway up the stairs. Elizabeth shook her head as she put away the rest of the groceries by herself. Her mind wandered back to Patrick and his problems. It didn't seem very fair that Patrick was so unhappy. She kept wondering if there was some way she could help him. But right now, she didn't have a single idea.

Two

◇

That Wednesday morning, Jessica searched among the crowded schoolyard for Lila Fowler.

"Lila," Jessica said when she finally found her. "Did you come up with a great idea for our science project?"

"Not yet, Jess, but I will," Lila replied, tossing her light brown hair behind her shoulders.

"We have science class first period. We'd better come up with something right now," Jessica said.

Lila flashed her cunning smile. "Don't worry so much, Jess. We don't have time now. I'll think of something during homeroom. Come on, let's go in."

"I'm going to wait for Elizabeth," Jessica muttered.

"Suit yourself," Lila replied as her eyes scanned the schoolyard for another Unicorn. "I'll go see if Ellen has come up with any ideas for a science project. She'd be fun to work with."

Jessica had to struggle to keep from screaming.

Lila made her so angry sometimes. She looked around at her schoolmates and was quickly distracted by Bruce Patman. Bruce was a seventh grader, and one of the cutest boys in the whole middle school, as well as one of the richest. In Jessica's book, that made him perfect.

"Hi, Bruce," Jessica said, walking up to him.

"Hey, Jess." He gave her a fleeting smile, but looked as if he was about to walk on.

"You're going to the concert, aren't you?" Jessica asked, trying to strike up a conversation.

The Wild Ones, a popular high school band, were scheduled to play out at Secca Lake on Saturday. The concert was a fund-raiser for the school library and all the money from ticket sales would go toward buying new books.

"I suppose so," Bruce said, sounding bored. "When is it, again?"

Jessica suspected Bruce already knew. He just had to live up to his reputation for being cool and casual. "It's this coming Saturday. They're supposed to give us the final details in homeroom."

Looking at Bruce's handsome profile, the wheels started turning in Jessica's brain. The Wild Ones were terrific, and this concert was going to be a major event. Wouldn't it be great to listen to the music sitting next to someone as cute and popular as Bruce?

Before Jessica could continue the conversation, the first bell rang. Bruce gave her a wave and walked away. Jessica stood looking after him for a few seconds, then hurried to her homeroom.

After Mr. Davis, her homeroom teacher, had taken attendance, he clapped his hands and said, "All right, gang, I have an announcement to make about this weekend's library fund-raiser. Tickets are three dollars each and anyone who wants to attend should meet in front of the school at six o'clock on Saturday. The buses will take you out and bring you back." Mr. Davis wrinkled his nose. "This is to be a rock concert, I believe." He looked down at the piece of paper the office had sent. "A group called the Wild Ones."

A buzz went around the classroom as kids whispered about the concert.

"All right, all right. Let's settle down, class," Mr. Davis commanded. Jessica barely heard him. She was too busy looking out the window, daydreaming about how special it would be to watch the sun set on the lake with Bruce Patman's arm around her.

As the bell rang for first period, Elizabeth came hurrying up to Jessica. "Jess, Patrick's not in school today. Maybe we should drop his homework assignments off at his house after school?"

"Sure," Jessica said, her mind still on the concert.

Elizabeth looked at her curiously. "What's up, Jessica?" She could always tell when her twin wasn't paying attention.

"Nothing." Jessica blushed, not wanting to share her romantic vision. "I—I was just thinking about my science project."

"Oh. Well, just be sure to copy down Patrick's homework assignments, OK?"

Jessica nodded and grabbed her books. Even though she preferred to think about Bruce, she knew she had better get to Mr. Siegal's class and see if Lila had come up with an idea yet.

As she sat down at her desk, Lila sauntered up and whispered one word to her. "Rainbows."

"Rainbows?" she replied, puzzled.

Lila nodded. "We'll do a chart on them. They'll be fun to draw because they're so pretty."

"Great," Jessica said, relieved. She never should have doubted Lila after all.

But when class began, Mr. Siegal had a shock for them. "I hope you've all been thinking about your projects," he said, looking around the room.

Everyone nodded.

"Well, I've been thinking about them, too." He ran a hand through his thick black hair. "It seems to me I see the same people working together over and over again. So this time, I've decided we're going to pick partners by drawing names out of a hat."

Everyone groaned, while Jessica and Lila exchanged horrified glances. They could get stuck with *anyone* now.

"Come on, it's not the end of the world," Mr. Siegal assured them. He lifted a tweed hat from behind his desk. "I've put all your names in here. We'll just go around the room until everyone has a partner."

Mr. Siegal started at the front of Jessica's row,

and each person read aloud the name they pulled out of the hat. Jessica touched several of the folded pieces of paper before taking out the one she felt was lucky. When she opened it and read the name, her face fell.

"Jessica, we're waiting for your partner's name," Mr. Siegal said.

She gulped. "Winston Egbert."

There were a few giggles and Jessica looked over at Lila who was making a face. Winston was tall and gangly, with big ears that turned bright red when he was embarrassed. Most of the time he was pretty quiet and he worked really hard in school. As far as Jessica was concerned, there was just one word for Winston Egbert: nerd!

Crumpling up the slip with Winston's name, Jessica turned around to see who Lila's partner would be. She hoped that Lila would get someone equally bad, but the smile on Lila's face made Jessica frown. "Ellen Riteman," Lila read approvingly from her slip of paper.

Jessica was furious. She couldn't remember a more unlucky day in her life when suddenly Mr. Siegal interrupted her thoughts.

"Class, I'm going to give you some time now to discuss project ideas with your partners. I know you're all creative, but try to be fair and choose the idea that's the most interesting. Please get up and find your partners now."

There was a great shuffle as everyone got up and moved around, but Jessica stayed in her seat. If

Winston Egbert wanted to talk to her, let him come over. She looked longingly toward the corner where Lila and Ellen were happily chatting away, about rainbows no doubt.

"Er . . . Jessica?"

Jessica looked up at Winston, looming over her desk. Sure enough, his ears were fire-engine red.

"Yes?" she said coldly, as if she had no idea what he wanted to talk to her about.

"I thought, uh, that we could, um, talk about the project?" he mumbled.

Jessica sighed. There was no way out of this. "OK."

"Did you have any ideas?" he asked politely.

"Not really," Jessica had to admit.

A hopeful smile lit Winston's face. "Then we can do my project."

Jessica knew Winston was very good in science. If she went along with his idea, maybe he'd do most of the work. "All right," she said, trying to sound a little more agreeable. "What is it?"

"I want to grow mold."

"Mold!" Jessica's eyes grew wide.

"You know. That kind of fungus stuff . . ."

"I know what mold is, Winston. It's gross!"

Winston's brow wrinkled. "It's really very interesting stuff, Jessica."

If Winston Egbert thought that she was going to have anything to do with mold, he was crazy. She shook her head violently. "No way."

"But it would make a great experiment," Winston told her. "You take pieces of bread and put them in different places. Then you record how fast the mold grows."

"That's disgusting!"

"We can even do a report on molds and penicillin. If we do a good job, we might even get into the science fair."

"The science fair? Really?" Jessica considered the possibility. It would certainly be impressive if she made it to the science fair. Elizabeth was usually the one who got all the honors. And Lila! Boy, would she be jealous. "Could we leave the pieces of bread at your house?" she asked cautiously.

"Sure," Winston said agreeably.

Well, at least that was settled. Jessica wouldn't have to worry about any of the Unicorns seeing moldy pieces of bread lying around her house. Mold certainly wasn't her favorite topic in the world, but there was nothing she could do about it now.

Jessica complained to Elizabeth all the way to Patrick's house after school. "Mold and Winston. What a combination."

"Oh, it won't be so bad," Elizabeth consoled. "It might even be interesting."

"The Unicorns are going to die laughing when they find out," Jessica said in an exaggerated tone.

"I don't know," Elizabeth said. "Maybe you could grow some *purple* mold." Purple was the Unicorns' favorite color and each member tried to wear something purple every day.

Jessica gave Elizabeth a dirty look. "Very funny."

"Well, here we are," Elizabeth said, stopping in front of Patrick's house.

The twins climbed the steps and rang the bell. Patrick looked through the window, and then opened the door. "Hi," he said, surprised.

"We brought your homework assignments. Are you feeling well enough for us to come in?" Elizabeth inquired.

"I was running a pretty high fever this morning, but I feel better now," Patrick said, not opening the door any wider.

"Can we come in?" Jessica asked in her usual blunt fashion.

"I'm not supposed to have more than one friend over at a time," Patrick told them, obviously embarrassed.

"Why not?" Elizabeth asked.

Patrick sighed. "It's another of Mom's new rules. She says three kids in the house are enough already. If I have friends over, it's extra work."

"Maybe we should go, then," Elizabeth said.

But Patrick motioned them into the house. "I guess it'll be all right. My mother took Brian to the dentist and I'm home with Joey."

Elizabeth looked around the Morris house. She hadn't been there for a very long time, but it still had the same cozy look she remembered. Nicely framed pictures hung on the faded wallpaper and bright green plants stood near every window. A pretty, striped afghan covered the slightly worn couch.

"Hi. Hi." A little boy who looked a lot like Patrick toddled up to the twins.

"Well, hello there," Elizabeth said, reaching down to ruffle Joey's hair. Jessica took a step backward. His hands were full of sticky red stuff she didn't want to get on her white blouse.

Elizabeth sat down on the couch, and pulled Joey onto her lap. "I brought your English book for you, Patrick. We have to read Chapter Three for tomorrow. Oh. And be ready for a pop quiz in the next day or so."

"And your science partner is Julie Porter. Mr. Siegal made us pick names out of a hat."

"Julie's nice," Patrick remarked. "She plays the flute, doesn't she?"

"Yes. Both of her parents are musicians, too. Her mother teaches music at Sweet Valley High and her father's a conductor," Elizabeth informed him.

"Wow," Patrick said, impressed.

"Sounds boring to me," Jessica said bluntly. "Anyway, here's your science homework." She handed him a worksheet.

They went over some other homework assignments and had just gotten around to showing Patrick their complicated math problems when they heard a car pulling into the gravel driveway. "Oh, no." Patrick's head jerked up from the math book. "My mother's home."

"Should we leave?" Elizabeth asked, a little panicked by the look on Patrick's face.

"One of you has to. My mom will kill me if she finds I've got two people over."

"I'll go," Jessica offered, jumping up. She didn't have any desire to see Patrick's mother.

"All right," Patrick said, "go out the back door."

Grabbing her books, Jessica followed Patrick into the large, old-fashioned kitchen. He pointed toward the door and then ran back into the living room where his mother and Brian were saying hello to Elizabeth.

Jessica was trying to unlock the kitchen door when she felt a sticky hand grab her leg. "Hi. Hi," little Joey jabbered. Trying to disengage herself, Jessica whispered frantically, "I've got to go, Joey."

Joey's face screwed up into a scowl. "Hi," he said, tears forming in his eyes.

"No, bye-bye. I've got to go bye-bye." Getting the door open at last, she dashed out just as Joey started to howl.

She had made it as far as the front of the house when she almost ran into Mrs. Morris who was back outside unloading groceries from the car.

"Elizabeth," Mrs. Morris said, sounding surprised. "How did you get out here so quickly?"

Jessica stood still, trying to think of a reply. "I . . . I guess I just move fast."

"Well, as long as you're out here, do you think you could help me take these inside?"

Jessica could see Patrick looking frantically out the living room window. She didn't see how she could refuse Mrs. Morris's request for help, so she nodded dumbly and walked over to the car. She was thankful that she and Elizabeth were both wearing their gym outfits. The white blouses and navy blue shorts weren't identical, but they matched closely enough.

"It was so nice of you to bring Patrick his homework," Mrs. Morris commented as she handed Jessica a large brown sack, and grabbed two for herself.

"No problem," Jessica said, keeping her head down so Mrs. Morris wouldn't notice the distinctive purple beaded necklace she was wearing. Elizabeth was wearing a gold heart on a chain.

As they turned the corner of the house to get to the back door, Jessica saw Elizabeth sneaking down the front steps. *Don't look around, Mrs. Morris,* Jessica prayed. If she did, there was no way she could miss Elizabeth.

Mrs. Morris continued to chatter away as she led Jessica up the back stairs and into the kitchen. Patrick was waiting for them, his face pale.

Mrs. Morris put the groceries down on the kitchen table and looked closely at Patrick. "Dear, you look peaked."

"I'm not feeling very well right now," Patrick admitted.

"Elizabeth, maybe you'd better go now so Patrick can get some rest."

"You're absolutely right, Mrs. Morris," Jessica said politely.

"Thanks for bringing over my homework," Patrick said, walking her to the door.

"We were glad to . . . I mean, I was."

Jessica heaved a sigh of relief as she closed the door behind her. *That's my last good deed for a long time,* she vowed, running across the Morrises' lawn to the sidewalk. *Leave it to Elizabeth and her helpful nature to cause trouble.*

Three

◆

"I don't get it," Elizabeth said, looking at her sister with confusion. "You want to borrow my green T-shirt even though it's dirty?"

"Yes. And those shorts you ripped the other day," Jessica added.

"But those shorts don't really match that T-shirt."

Jessica stretched out on her sister's navy-and-white bedspread. "I know."

"Are you feeling all right, Jess?" Elizabeth asked with concern. "You usually only borrow my best stuff. Why in the world do you want my worst clothes?"

"I want to wear them when Winston comes over."

The twins were having a long weekend off from school because of a special teachers' conference. Jessica had reluctantly made plans with Winston Egbert to get started on the mold project. She had decided that the worse she looked the less time Winston would want to spend with her. Certainly, she didn't want Winston to think she would dress up for him.

Elizabeth put her hands on her hips. "That's kind of silly, isn't it, Jess? Even if you don't like Winston . . ."

Jessica waved away her sister's objections. "I wouldn't waste anything I have in my closet on Winston. Besides, we're going to be growing mold, for goodness sakes. What if I drop some on me?"

Elizabeth laughed. "All right." She went into the bathroom connecting their rooms and rummaged around in the hamper. "Here you go," she said, tossing a wrinkled T-shirt at Jessica.

"Thanks." Jessica picked up the T-shirt from the edge of the bed where it had fallen.

"And here are the shorts," Elizabeth said.

Jessica spread the shorts out in front of her. Elizabeth was right, the colors really clashed, but she was relieved to see the tear in the shorts was only around the pocket. She didn't want to look like a complete ragamuffin.

Nevertheless, when Steven caught sight of her at breakfast, he burst into laughter. "Did you sleep in that outfit?" he inquired.

"She's just making a fashion statement," Elizabeth answered, helping herself to some milk.

"Yeah? What's the statement? 'I love these creases to pieces'?" Steven loved to laugh at his own jokes.

"You're not exactly the best-dressed boy at Sweet Valley High," Jessica snapped.

Steven ran a hand through his dark brown hair. "That's not what the girls tell me."

"Well, they should see the way you throw your clothes all over the bedroom," Jessica replied slyly. "In fact, maybe I should take a picture of your bedroom and pass it around."

"Go ahead," Steven replied. "I dare you."

Before the banter could escalate into a full-blown argument, Mr. Wakefield entered the kitchen, ready to go to his law office. "So, what are you lucky kids doing on the start of your long weekend?" he asked.

"I'm going to be working on my science project," Jessica said virtuously.

"That's great, honey," Mr. Wakefield said with obvious approval. "I'm glad you're taking it seriously. What about you, Elizabeth?"

"I don't have much homework, so I thought I'd invite some friends over to go swimming."

Mr. Wakefield raised his eyebrow. "Without an adult home? You know the rules."

"Mom's coming home early today. I'll watch them till then," Steven interjected, swallowing the last of his toast. He had received his Red Cross certificate at the end of the summer.

"That's not fair. If I had known you were going to have a pool party, I would never have made arrangements with Winston."

"Perhaps you'll finish up early and then you can join them," Mr. Wakefield said. "Elizabeth, why don't you phone your mother at the office and make sure it's all right with her? She had to go to work early today."

"OK, Dad. Then I'll call Amy and Julie if Mom says it's OK."

Jessica spent the rest of the morning half-heartedly cleaning her room by moving piles of clothing from one spot to another. Along the way she threw out a few candy wrappers and wadded up pieces of notebook paper. She glanced around the room critically. It looked a little better. Flopping down on her newly-made bed, Jessica thought gloomily that this wonderful free day was about to be wasted. Why hadn't she been the one to plan a pool party with her friends? She could even have invited Bruce over. But when the doorbell rang she resigned herself to Winston's company.

By the time she got downstairs, Winston was already inside, talking to Elizabeth. "But I didn't bring a bathing suit," he was saying.

"E-liz-a-beth!" Jessica's message was clear, but her sister ignored her.

"That's all right," Elizabeth told Winston. "We have plenty of old suits around. I'm sure we can find one that fits you."

"OK," Winston said happily. "I guess I can stick around."

Jessica rolled her eyes. It was a good thing she hadn't invited any friends over after all. She certainly didn't want any of the Unicorns to see Winston lounging in her backyard.

"We'd better get started," she said sharply.

"Right." He peered at Jessica. "Hey, that's a nice T-shirt. I have one the same color."

Elizabeth placed both hands over her mouth to stifle a giggle. "Let's go into the den," Jessica said, trying to maintain her dignity.

"Uh, I've got a little bad news, Jessica," Winston said apologetically.

"We can't do mold?" she asked hopefully.

"Oh, we can grow it, but we have to do it over here. My mom is redecorating and the painters are tearing the house up."

"Winston," Jessica screeched. "I don't want pieces of moldy bread all over my house."

Winston shrugged helplessly. "I don't see any way around it. The bread might accidentally get thrown out at my place, and then we wouldn't have a project."

Visions of winning a blue ribbon at the science fair danced in Jessica's head. "All right," she said, finally giving in. "What do we have to do?"

Winston explained that pieces of bread would be placed in different spots around the house—in a hot, sunny window, in the dank basement—wherever there were differences in light and temperature. Then they would chart how quickly mold grew in each environment.

When he was done, Jessica had only one question. "Are you sure we'll win first prize at the science fair?" She didn't want to get involved with this experiment unless she had some guarantees.

"Wait a minute." Winston held up a hand. "I

didn't say anything about winning first prize. But between our display and our report on penicillin, we'll have a good chance of getting in."

"Then let's get the bread," Jessica sighed.

By the time they finished placing the bread around the house and making their first notes, the pool party was in full swing. Elizabeth and Amy Sutton, one of Elizabeth's best friends, were splashing in the above-ground pool. Steven was reading a book in the lounge chair while Julie Porter sat talking to Patrick Morris.

"Hi, Patrick," Jessica said, surprised. "I didn't know you were coming over."

Patrick shaded his eyes and looked up. "Elizabeth called and since I finished all my homework in the morning, my mother said I could come over and talk to Julie about our science project."

"Well, that's good," Jessica said. "Did you decide on anything?"

"We're going to explain sound waves," Julie replied.

"And show how musical instruments like the saxophone and flute work," Patrick said, sounding excited.

"Mr. Siegal should like that," Jessica said eagerly, although she was secretly relieved it wasn't quite as intriguing as growing mold.

"Hey, Winston, why don't you get into your suit," Patrick suggested. "You, too, Jessica. Then we can have a game of water volleyball."

Winston looked inquiringly at Jessica, his ears burning a little. "Uh, Elizabeth said . . ."

"Right. Come on. I'll find you a suit," Jessica said in a curt tone. She led Winston back into the house.

"Poor Jessica," Julie said. "I don't think she likes playing hostess to her science partner."

Julie and Patrick were still talking about their sound-wave project when Elizabeth climbed out of the pool.

"You guys have picked a great topic for your science project."

"Yeah," Julie agreed. "And it's especially good for us since we're both so interested in music."

"I didn't know you were a musician, Patrick," Elizabeth commented.

"I'm not, exactly. But I'm thinking of trying out for the school band." Patrick rubbed his knuckles nervously. "I've been trying to teach myself how to play the saxophone for a while but I haven't gotten very far. I have a friend at a different school who used to let me play his sometimes."

"That's great!" Elizabeth exclaimed.

"Well, maybe. But I'm not sure my parents will give me permission to join the band."

"Sure they will," Julie said confidently. "Parents like it when their kids are interested in music."

"Your parents, maybe. But that's because they're musicians, too," Patrick said.

"Speaking of music, I can hardly wait until the

concert tomorrow," Elizabeth said excitedly. "The Wild Ones have such great songs."

Just then Winston wandered out to the pool wearing an old bathing suit of Steven's. He kept hitching up the red trunks to make sure they didn't slip off of his skinny frame. "I hear the tickets are just about sold out."

Amy, toweling herself off, joined the group. "Well, I have mine. What about you guys?"

Everyone said they did, except Patrick. "I . . . I'm not sure I can go."

"Why not?" Julie asked, surprised.

Fortunately, at that moment the group was distracted by the ringing of the doorbell. "I'll get it," Jessica called from inside the kitchen.

She opened the door wide, and to her shock there stood Lila, Ellen, Aaron Dallas, and Bruce Patman. "What are you guys doing here?"

Lila took in Jessica's outfit in a glance. "The filter in my pool went out and Bruce's pool is being cleaned, so we were wondering if we could swim here."

Jessica tried to smooth the wrinkles out of her shirt. "Well, I don't know," she stalled. She certainly didn't want her friends to see the group Elizabeth had assembled at the pool. "Uh, my parents aren't home, so maybe it's not a good idea."

"Oh, that's too bad," Lila said grumpily.

"Maybe we should just head over to the mall and get some lunch. I'm hungry," Ellen said.

"Do you want to meet us there?" Lila asked. "I

don't want to wait while you change," she added pointedly.

"Yeah, maybe I'll join you," Jessica said weakly as she closed the door and leaned against it. She couldn't believe it. An afternoon with Bruce blown. And he had seen her looking like a total mess. *Winston Egbert!* she thought. *This is all his fault.*

The next evening the twins were still arguing. "Jessica, I can't believe you're blaming Winston. He didn't exactly force you to wear my shirt and shorts."

Jessica was standing at Elizabeth's closet, hoping to find something to wear to the Wild Ones concert. "You never stick up for me, Liz. That's not very sisterly."

"I stick up for you way too much," Elizabeth said, defending herself. "And why are you showing such interest in my closet?"

"I was just wondering what you were going to wear to the concert."

"What *I* was going to wear? Or what *you* were going to wear?" Elizabeth questioned sharply.

"OK, OK, I admit it," Jessica confessed. "Your blue blouse would look great with my jeans."

Elizabeth shook her head. "Forget it, Jess. I'm wearing that blouse. Anyway, just remember what happened the last time you wore my clothes. You were humiliated."

Jessica decided to give up and was on her way back to her own room when Elizabeth said, "By the way, I want to stop at Patrick's house before we head over to school."

"Patrick?" Jessica said with surprise. "I thought he wasn't going. Besides, all the tickets are sold out."

Elizabeth grabbed a ticket off her dresser. "Mrs. Sutton dropped this by earlier. Amy's sick and can't go, so she said Patrick could buy her ticket if he wanted."

Jessica shrugged. "All right, we can stop. But let's make sure we leave early. I don't want to miss the bus at school. It's leaving exactly at six." She hadn't told any of the Unicorns about her plan to spend the evening with Bruce, but she was sure she could make it happen.

Allowing themselves plenty of time, the twins made their way to Patrick's house. Elizabeth marched up the stairs and rang the front doorbell. When Mrs. Morris finally appeared at the door, the twins noticed that her eyes were red, as if she had been crying. "Yes, girls. What is it?"

The twins looked at each other. She certainly wasn't being very friendly.

"I have an extra ticket for the concert. The one out at the lake?"

"Didn't Patrick tell you he couldn't go?" Mrs. Morris cut her short.

"Well, yes, but we hoped he'd change his mind. The ticket is only three dollars," Elizabeth said.

"It's a fund-raiser," Jessica chimed in. "To raise money for library books."

"That's very nice, but I'm sorry. It's just not possible." She started to close the door.

"Will you tell Patrick we came by?" Elizabeth asked.

"Certainly," Mrs. Morris replied. Then she shut the door.

"I can't understand why Patrick isn't allowed to go," Elizabeth said. "I hope his mother at least tells him we were here."

"She won't have to," Jessica said, as she moved quickly down the stairs and across the yard.

"What do you mean?" Elizabeth asked, rushing to keep up with her sister.

"I saw him looking out his bedroom window."

Elizabeth whirled around and glanced up at the second story window. Patrick was still there, looking dejected. He shrugged his shoulders as if to say, "See what I mean?"

"I can't believe how mean Mrs. Morris is. She was barely polite to us," Jessica said in disbelief.

"Oh, come on, Jess. She wasn't *that* bad."

But Jessica's eyes were hard as she marched toward school. "For all we know, she may be keeping Patrick prisoner in there!"

"That's silly," Elizabeth said, but deep down she was just as worried about Patrick.

When they arrived at school, the yard was swarming with kids waiting to pile into the buses. Jessica wanted to sneak into the seventh-grade bus so she could sit with Bruce, but the homeroom teachers were all watching carefully, so she was forced to ride with the rest of the sixth graders. But she wasted no time when they arrived at Secca Lake. She jumped off the bus and began to scan the crowd for Bruce.

"Jessica, do you want to sit with Julie and me?" Elizabeth asked.

"No thanks. I've got my own blanket. I'm going to find some of the Unicorns." She headed off in the direction of Lila and Ellen, but when she noticed Bruce and a couple of his friends putting down their blanket, she boldly placed her gray cotton blanket right behind theirs. Bruce had to notice her now, she thought with satisfaction.

"Hey, Blondie," Bruce said, turning in her direction while the band was warming up. "Why are you sitting all by yourself?"

Jessica was sure Bruce was just about to ask her to join him. "It seemed like a good place to see the show," she shrugged.

"Did you have a fight with your friends?"

Jessica frowned. "No, of course not."

"You mean you want to sit alone?" he asked, puzzled.

Now Jessica could feel her face reddening. "Of course not. I, uh, just couldn't find any of the Unicorns."

"There's a whole bunch of them over there," Bruce said, pointing to his left.

Jessica looked in the Unicorns' direction and saw Lila and Ellen already applauding as the band warmed up. "Oh, thank you." Trying to maintain her dignity, Jessica gathered her blanket and headed toward her friends. At least Bruce had talked to her. He was probably just too embarrassed to invite her to sit with him in front of his friends.

"Where have you been?" Lila asked, barely taking her eyes off the stage as Jessica spread her blanket beside Lila's.

"Nowhere," Jessica said with a sigh. "Nowhere at all."

Four

◇

"So, how was the concert?" Patrick asked Elizabeth at lunch on Monday.

"It was terrific," she said. "The Wild Ones were great. They played six encores. By the end everyone was jumping up and dancing."

"Sounds great," Patrick said glumly.

There was an awkward silence. Elizabeth examined the remains of her peanut-butter sandwich as if it was the most interesting thing in the world. Finally she said, "I'm sorry you couldn't make it."

"You had an extra ticket, didn't you?"

"Yes. Amy got sick and she gave us her ticket for you."

"My folks had already said no."

"But why?" Elizabeth couldn't help asking.

Patrick crumpled up his brown paper lunch bag. "They didn't want to extend my curfew," he said angrily.

Elizabeth felt bad for Patrick, but she didn't know what to say to make him feel better. Life at the Wakefields' was so different.

"I just hope they're going to let me join the band," he said, calming down a little. "Last year they said I probably could."

"Well, you see, things aren't so bad." Elizabeth couldn't imagine any parent not wanting a child to get involved with music.

"But that was last year. They don't let me do anything anymore."

"The first band meeting is today, isn't it?" she asked, wondering if he planned to attend.

Patrick looked up at the lunchroom clock. "Yes. It's in a few minutes. I think I'll get over there a little early and talk to Ms. McDonald," he said, getting up to leave.

The airy music room was filled with music stands and sheet music when Patrick walked in, but Ms. McDonald, the music teacher and bandleader, was nowhere to be seen. He spotted Julie Porter sitting in a corner with her flute, though, and he walked over to talk to her.

"Hi, Julie," he said. "Do you know how Ms. McDonald is going to conduct this meeting?"

"Well, if it's the same as last year, she'll divide us into two groups—kids who already own an instrument and those who don't."

"I haven't got a saxaphone," he told her.

"If you don't have your own instrument, the school will loan you one."

"That's great," Patrick said happily.

The classroom started filling up with potential band members and soon the room was alive with toots, hums, and plinks. Ms. McDonald breezed in, smiling. "I'm glad to see I have such an enthusiastic group here. Why don't we get settled and I'll tell you what's going to happen."

As Julie guessed, Ms. McDonald quickly put the instrument owners into one group and those without into another. Then she distributed available instruments to those who needed them.

"I'm going to give you something very easy to practice," she informed them as she passed out sheet music. "It's the Sweet Valley song and it only has a few notes." She spent time with each student, demonstrating the fingering position of each note.

Ms. McDonald patted Patrick on the shoulder after he ran through the notes on his saxophone. "Keep practicing and you'll have it down in no time," she said, smiling at him.

"When are the tryouts held?" he asked anxiously.

"Next Monday. The band will play the following Saturday at the middle-school football game against the Cougars."

"Next week, huh," Patrick said uncertainly. It sounded so soon.

"Don't worry, this is very easy," she told him. "Just keep practicing."

But Patrick was worried, and not about learning to play the song. At the close of the school day he stood in front of his locker trying to decide whether or not to bring his saxophone home. He knew he needed to practice, but he wasn't sure how his parents would react if he told them he was trying out for the band. They had been so negative about everything lately.

He stroked the shiny sax—it had a few scratches, but Patrick thought it was the most beautiful instrument in the world. Reluctantly, he put it back into its leather case and slammed his locker shut. He'd better talk to his parents first.

Patrick and his mother were in the kitchen preparing dinner when Mr. Morris came home, looking tired. His job as foreman of a construction crew often made him weary by the end of the day. "What time is supper?" he asked.

"It will be ready any minute," Mrs. Morris said.

When Patrick had finished making a salad, he took his five-year-old brother, Brian, into the living room for a private talk. "Brian, I want you to do something for me. Try to be good during dinner."

Brian screwed his face up into a puzzled expression. "I'm always good."

"I know," Patrick said, patting his head. "But tonight, try to be extra good. Don't spill your milk or anything."

"It's Joey who spills his milk," Brian insisted, his voice getting shrill.

"Yeah, you're right. How about helping me make sure that *Joey* doesn't do anything bad?" he suggested, using a bit of reverse psychology.

"We'll both watch Joey, right?" Brian said with a smile, before popping his thumb into his mouth.

Patrick knew it was important to have a nice peaceful meal. His parents would be in a better mood and might be more receptive to his request about the band. Dinner went smoothly. Patrick even cleared the table without being asked.

"You've been awfully quiet tonight, Patrick. Is something wrong?" his mother asked, concerned.

Patrick sat down again and fidgeted in his chair. "There is something I wanted to ask you."

"Well, what is it, Patrick?" Mr. Morris asked.

"I want to join the school band," Patrick answered boldly.

His parents exchanged looks. "I know you've always been interested in the saxophone. . . ." his mother began.

"I am, Mom. I really want to learn how to play it well. Last year when we talked about it, you said I could."

"We made no promises," his mother fretted.

"But you said—"

"Lessons! Lessons cost lots of money, Patrick," his father said.

"I don't have to take private lessons. The school—"

"You spend too much time with your ear stuck to your radio now," Mr. Morris interrupted without letting Patrick finish.

Mrs. Morris got up and nervously began wiping

the crumbs off the table with her napkin. "You've got to study, Pat. Music would take up too much time."

"That's right," Mr. Morris agreed emphatically. "The most important thing for a boy your age is to keep your grades up, and you can't do that if you're involved with a lot of extracurricular activities."

"I could do both," Patrick cried. "I know I could."

His father shook his head. "We can't take that chance, Patrick. We're counting on you to set a good example for Joey and Brian. That's all there is to it."

"Your dad's right," Mrs. Morris agreed. "There're a lot of reasons we can't say yes, but your grades are the main one."

"What other reasons?" Patrick demanded sharply.

"I said that's all there is to it," Mr. Morris said, raising his voice. "And don't talk back to your mother."

"All right, just forget it!" Patrick stormed away from the table and ran to the room he shared with Brian. "Go away," he yelled at his brother, who had followed him upstairs. Brian looked at him with frightened eyes, then scampered out.

Flopping down on his bed, Patrick stared up at the crack in the ceiling. What was going on? His parents had always been strict, insisting that as the oldest child, he had to set a good example, but they usually explained their decisions to him. Lately, they had just been saying no to everything, flat out. And they got so angry if he tried to argue.

He had been upset about missing the Wild Ones concert, but compared to this disappointment, that was nothing. Not being allowed to try out for the band was really a blow.

Patrick rolled over on his side. He wasn't going to give in that easily. Somehow he was going to prove to his parents that he could be in the band *and* keep up with his schoolwork. Then they'd see they were wrong. They just had to.

By the next morning, Patrick was feeling much better. He had come up with a plan. Whistling a little, he walked into the kitchen, and his mother gave him a relieved smile. "I'm glad to see you're in a better mood this morning, Patrick."

His mother looked tired in her housedress and slippers. Patrick wondered if he should abandon his plan. He didn't want to make his parents unhappy. But he wanted to play in the band so badly. He would be disobeying his parents, but he was certain they would be really proud of him once they saw how much he could accomplish. "Yeah, Mom, I'm in a much better mood."

Hurrying through breakfast, he walked as quickly as he could over to the twins' house. They were the key to getting his plan under way.

When Patrick knocked at the kitchen door, he could see the whole Wakefield family sitting around the table, laughing.

"Hey, Pat, how you doin'?" Steven greeted him, as he walked in.

"Would you like to have some breakfast with us?" Mrs. Wakefield asked graciously.

"I just ate, thanks."

"We have to be going anyway," Jessica said, getting up.

"OK, girls. Enjoy your day at school," Mr. Wakefield said. The twins gathered their books and followed Patrick out the door.

"What's up, Patrick?" Elizabeth asked as soon as they were outside.

Patrick told Elizabeth and Jessica what had happened with his parents the previous night.

"That's awful," Jessica said. "And it's not fair."

"Couldn't you talk to your parents one more time?" Elizabeth asked. "Maybe they didn't understand how important being in the band is to you."

Patrick shook his head. "They're never going to agree unless they see with their own eyes that I can do it."

"So what are you going to do?" Jessica asked.

"Well, if it's OK, I want to hide my saxophone at your house."

"But what good will that do?" a confused Elizabeth wondered aloud.

"I'll come over whenever I can and practice," Patrick explained. "The song isn't that hard. I should have it down in no time."

"What a great idea," Jessica said enthusiastically.

"I don't know, Patrick. I'm not sure it's such a good idea," Elizabeth said.

"Why not?" her sister demanded.

Elizabeth knew how much the band meant to Patrick, but lying to his parents didn't seem right. But before she could explain her concern, he went on.

"All I need is a chance, Elizabeth. I want to prove I can handle both band practice *and* schoolwork."

"After all, Lizzie, we're really only giving Patrick an opportunity to make his parents proud of him."

Patrick and Jessica spent the rest of the walk to school trying to convince Elizabeth that hiding the saxophone was OK. When they reached the front entrance to Sweet Valley Middle School, she finally agreed. "All right. I suppose we can hide the saxophone. For a while at least."

"I knew I could count on you both," Patrick said ecstatically.

Once he had disappeared into the schoolyard, Elizabeth turned toward Jessica. "I hope you know what you're getting us into, Jess."

"What's wrong with helping a friend?"

"Is that what we're doing?"

"I don't believe it, Elizabeth. You're the one who's always telling me I don't help people enough. Now when I try to do something for Patrick, you think it's wrong. It's not as if we're committing a crime or something." She shook her head. "Boy, there's absolutely no satisfying you."

Elizabeth had to admit what Jessica said made sense. It was true she was always reminding her sister to be more considerate and helpful. But she had the feeling that helping Patrick Morris wasn't going to be as easy as Jessica made it seem.

Five

◇

"I like Patrick," Steven said, turning on the TV in the den, "but how long do we have to listen to him making those duck sounds on the saxophone? It's Friday, and he's been at it since Tuesday."

Elizabeth looked at her brother hopefully. "He's getting better, don't you think?"

"Sure," Steven admitted. "But what's he doing over here anyway? Why doesn't he practice at his own house?"

This was the question Elizabeth had hoped she could avoid for several days. The whole thing was getting so complicated. Patrick sneaked over to the Wakefields' every free moment he could—usually before school, and sometimes even after.

In the morning, he tried to wait until Mr. and Mrs. Wakefield left for work, but if they were home, he went directly to the toolshed in the backyard to practice. Mr. and Mrs. Wakefield could hear the saxophone, but they assumed it was coming from a neighbor's house.

Elizabeth was relieved when Jessica walked into the den before she had to answer Steven's question. But Steven wasn't finished. "I was just telling your sister I'm tired of listening to Patrick tooting here all the time." He made a face. "And another thing—I'm not crazy about practically stepping on pieces of moldy bread every time I turn around."

"Then watch where you walk," Jessica informed him. "They're there for the good of science."

"They'd look better in the garbage pail. And they may just wind up there," he said darkly.

"Don't you dare!" Jessica squealed.

"Well, all I know is, between mold and sour notes, this house is getting to be a very unpleasant place to live."

The twins looked at each other. Elizabeth seemed tempted to tell Steven what was going on with Patrick, but Jessica shook her head. The fewer people who knew they were aiding Patrick against his parents' wishes, the better.

"I'll be handing in my science project next week," Jessica said. "And you'll be proud of me when I win a blue ribbon at the science fair."

Steven turned his attention back to the basketball game on television.

"Why don't we go outside?" Elizabeth said to her sister. "Maybe Patrick's ready to take a break."

"I hope so," Steven muttered as the twins left the room.

But when they reached the toolshed, Patrick was still tootling away.

"You've gotten so much better, Patrick," Jessica told him.

A red-faced Patrick wiped his brow. "Do you think so? I only have a few more days to practice."

"Jessica's right," Elizabeth assured him. "You sound great."

"Thanks," Patrick said with relief. "Cramming in practice sessions has been rough. I just hope I make the band so it's all worth it."

"Have your parents noticed you've been away from the house?" Elizabeth inquired.

"Not really. I just say I'm going to the library to study after school. Actually, I have been spending some time there. Julie and I worked hard to finish our science project early so I could spend more time practicing."

"Well, it's all for a good cause," Jessica assured him.

"Well, I hope so. Hey, here comes Winston," Patrick said, waving him over.

"It must be time for another mold check," Jessica said with a groan.

Sure enough, as soon as Winston was close enough to be heard, he yelled, "Jessica, time for the mold."

"Will you be quiet?" Jessica hissed when he was almost upon them. "We don't have to let the whole neighborhood know about this."

Patrick and Elizabeth broke up with laughter,

but Jessica was stony-faced. "Let's go inside so you can take our notes," she said crossly.

Winston had been careful to chart the progress of the moldy bread. He had purchased a thick lab notebook and came over regularly to write down what the mold looked like and how fast it was growing. As far as Jessica was concerned there was too much mold, and too much Winston. The only lucky break was that, so far, she had had to do little more than follow Winston around. He had even done most of the research for their written penicillin report.

As usual, they started in the basement where Winston had placed two pieces of bread, one on the window sill, the other in a dark corner. Winston picked up the piece of bread on the sill and held it up to the light coming from the window. "It's growing well," he announced.

Jessica wrinkled her nose. "What an ugly shade of green."

"You know, Jessica," Winston said, putting back the bread, "we have to think of a way to present this project."

"Present it? What do you mean?" she asked, following him to the dark corner where the other piece of bread sat in a dish.

Winston examined the bread and made notes in his notebook. "Well, think about it, Jessica. We can't just hand Mr. Siegal ten pieces of moldy bread."

Jessica had to admit that Winston was right. As they climbed the stairs and headed into the kitchen to check on another piece of bread in the refrigerator, she asked, "So, how do you want to present it?"

Winston turned to face her, a nervous look on his face. "I think you have to make some kind of display for them."

"Me! Why me?"

"You're more artistic than I am," he replied defensively. "Besides, I've been doing most of the work."

So he had *noticed*, Jessica thought. "This whole mold thing was your idea," she pouted.

"And it's a good one." Winston stood his ground. "You just have to come up with a way to display the project. And one more thing. I've done my share of the research for the penicillin report, so I'll give you the notes and you can write it up."

"What?" Jessica cried. "You can't dump everything on me. After all, I donated my house for this moldy project."

Winston looked at her steadily and then said, "So far you've done zilch, Jessica. Either write the report and make the display, or I'm taking credit for the whole thing. Then you'll be left without a science project."

Jessica's jaw dropped. She had never heard Winston Egbert sound quite so decisive.

"Don't forget, we need all this done by Monday," he added firmly.

Jessica moaned and groaned all weekend, but she wrote the report. She also got some Styrofoam fruit platters from the grocery store. On Sunday, she gathered up each slice of bread, placed it on a platter, covered it with plastic wrap, and then pasted on the labels she had made. She hated every moment of it. At least Winston had promised to help carry the finished product to school.

Elizabeth stuck her head into Jessica's room before breakfast on Monday morning. "Big day today. Are you ready to go?"

"Almost," Jessica said as she put a butterfly clip into her hair. "It's M-day," she added, smiling. "Mold and music."

Elizabeth giggled. "What a combination."

"I'm sure that Patrick is going to make the band," Jessica said, gathering her school books. "He's really been sounding great the last couple of days."

"You're right," Elizabeth agreed. "He's been practicing so hard. I'd feel terrible if he didn't make it."

"Don't worry. Both Patrick and I will be lucky today. And we'll deserve it, after what we've each been through," Jessica said.

When the twins clattered downstairs they saw both Winston, and Patrick waiting in the kitchen. Steven was finishing his breakfast and discussing the chances of the Sweet Valley Middle School football team with the two boys.

"They're good," Patrick assured him. "I'll have a front row seat . . . if I make the band, that is."

"You will," Steven said with conviction. "You're sounding good. And believe me, if anyone is in a position to know about your progress, it's me."

The twins, Winston, and Patrick set off to school.

Elizabeth was glad to see Patrick looking happy for a change. Winston was excited, too. Even Jessica looked eager to get to school.

Only when the first period bell rang did Jessica begin to feel nervous. Seeing Lila and Ellen's beautiful chart explaining rainbows didn't help to boost her confidence.

Sure enough, Lila peeked into Jessica's shopping bag as soon as she brought it into Mr. Siegal's room.

"Eww! Is that it?" she said, holding her nose.

"There isn't enough mold for it to smell," Jessica said frostily. It was one thing for her to think the mold was creepy, but no one else had the right to ridicule her project.

To Jessica's immense satisfaction, Mr. Siegal lingered the longest over the mold display when he made his rounds to inspect the projects. "Excellent," he said, leafing through Winston's copious notes. "You've really followed through on this. And the penicillin report is a nice tie-in."

"Thank you," Jessica said modestly.

"When are you going to make the recommendation for the science fair?" Winston asked.

"In a couple of days," Mr. Siegal answered, patting Winston on the shoulder.

"I think we're in," Winston whispered as soon as the teacher had walked by.

"Science fair, here we come," Jessica said excitedly. With a shock she realized that she was talking to Winston as if he was her friend. It made her feel strange.

"I hope Patrick has the same luck today," Winston commented. "Me, too," answered Jessica with a smile.

Band tryouts were held during lunch period. The music room was filled with prospective musicians, but Patrick tried not to let that bother him.

"Well, Patrick." Ms. McDonald smiled at him from her seat at the back of the room. "Are you ready?"

Patrick wiped his hand nervously on his pant leg. "I guess so."

"Then please begin," Ms. McDonald said, "and play your song through twice, so I can really get a feel for how you sound."

Patrick put every ounce of skill he had into his performance. His hours of practice seemed to be paying off. He didn't make one mistake and the second play-through was even livelier than the first.

There was applause when he finished. "Excellent," Ms. McDonald said. "I think you've put in a lot of hard work, plus you've got a good deal of natural talent. You've definitely made it, Pat."

Patrick spent a happy afternoon receiving congratulations from his friends. The twins were especially delighted.

"I knew you could do it, Patrick." Elizabeth was grinning from ear to ear.

"You're going to be the best saxophone player the band has ever had," Jessica said, slapping him on the back.

On his way home, Patrick began to worry. Everyone at school had been so glad for him but how would his parents react?

When he opened the screen door, he was surprised to see his father sitting in his worn leather chair reading the newspaper.

"Dad, what are you doing home?" Patrick asked with surprise.

Mr. Morris looked embarrassed. "Uh, there was a little less work than usual on the construction site today, so everyone went home early."

"How was school?" Mrs. Morris asked, wiping her hands on a towel as she came in from the kitchen.

"OK. Actually, it was pretty good."

"Did you get a good grade on a test or something?" Mr. Morris asked eagerly.

Patrick took a seat. "No. It was something else."

His parents looked at him expectantly.

"There were band tryouts today," he said, swallowing loudly. "And I made it."

"The band!" His father exploded. "I thought we made it clear. No band."

"I know, but that was because you didn't think I could keep up with my schoolwork and be in the band, too," Patrick said quickly.

"That's exactly right." Mr. Morris's voice was firm.

"Well, I did it."

"Did what, Patrick?" his mother said with a worried look.

"I practiced the saxophone all week and I managed to do all my homework, too. I got a hundred on my social studies test, and an eighty on my math test. That's the best I've gotten all year. Plus, I finished my science project three days before it was due."

Mr. Morris's face grew red. "You deliberately disobeyed me."

"I know, Dad, but I was sure if you saw that I could handle both, you'd let me join the band," Patrick said desperately.

"Patrick, that wasn't the way to go about it," Mrs. Morris said sadly.

"It certainly wasn't," Mr. Morris added. Patrick had never heard him sound so angry.

Patrick began to grow angry, too. "What else was I supposed to do? You wouldn't even give me a real reason for not letting me try out. You're not being fair," he cried. "Last year you said I could join the band."

"We said maybe," his mother informed him. "And that was last year."

"But Mom—"

"Patrick—" his father began.

"Please, can't we just sit down and talk this out quietly?" Mrs. Morris pleaded. "There's nothing to talk about, Jean," Mr. Morris answered. "Patrick simply can't be in the band."

"I played well today." Patrick's voice trembled dangerously. "It's an honor to be in the band."

His mother tried to put her arm around Patrick, but he pulled away. "I'm sorry, honey," was all she said.

"Oh, sure," Patrick said bitterly. "You don't care how I feel."

"That's it, young man," his father said, standing up. "Go to your room, right now!"

"Fine," Patrick yelled. "Who wants to stay in here with you!" He dashed to his room and slammed the door. As he lay on his bed, tears came to his eyes. He hated them! How could they be so cruel?

Maybe he couldn't be in the band, he thought, but he was going to make his parents sorry about their decision. Someday they were going to wish they hadn't been so unfair.

Six

◇

"Winston, Jessica, I have some very good news for you," Mr. Siegal said after school on Tuesday. "I'm glad you could spare me a few minutes this afternoon."

Ever since Mr. Siegal asked to see them earlier that day, Jessica had been excited. She was sure it meant that Mr. Siegal had selected their project for the district science fair.

She had grabbed Elizabeth in the hall between second and third period to tell her the good news. At lunch Jessica had boasted to a group of Unicorns, including Lila and Ellen, that it looked as if she was going to be representing Sweet Valley Middle School in the fair.

Now, standing here in Mr. Siegal's room, she could barely wait to hear the official announcement. "What is it, Mr. Siegal?" Jessica asked excitedly. "Are we going to be in the science fair?"

Mr. Siegal looked surprised. "Is that why you

thought I asked you here? I'm sorry. I didn't mean to raise your hopes about that."

"You mean you haven't chosen us?" Winston asked.

"No. I'm sorry. I haven't. I've given you both an A for your project, but Peter Burns's replica of a computer is our school's official entry."

Jessica and Winston exchanged disappointed looks. "Oh," Jessica said. "What is it you wanted to tell us?" she asked.

"The public library is having a Science Day. A famous author of children's science books is going to be there, and the library called to see if I could provide some exhibits. Along with Peter's project I thought of yours. It's extremely interesting, and of course, very visual."

All that fuzzy mold, Jessica thought. It was visual all right. But now that her hopes for the science fair were dashed, she didn't feel like showing it off.

"I guess it would be an honor to exhibit our project at the library on Science Day," Winston said slowly.

"Yes, it would. I hope I can count on you both to be there. There'll be many people attending and I'm sure you'll have a lot of questions to answer."

Jessica felt trapped. She really didn't care about standing around the library with her mold, but she could tell Mr. Siegal would be very unhappy if she didn't do it.

"I'll go," Winston said.

"I guess I will, too," Jessica shrugged. "When is it?"

"On Saturday. The librarian only got the idea to add exhibits this morning. A few of the seventh- and eighth-grade science classes will be represented, too."

"*This* Saturday," Jessica protested. "There's a football game that day."

Mr. Siegal looked at Jessica steadily. "Is that a problem?"

"I . . . guess not."

"Good. Then, I'll expect you both to be there on Saturday. I'll notify the librarian."

As soon as Jessica and Winston had left the science room and were out of earshot, Jessica let out a loud sigh. "I can't believe I'm going to miss the football game. Mr. Siegal just about forced us to say yes."

"Well, it's still a big deal, Jessica, even if it isn't the science fair."

"If you believe that, Winston, then maybe you wouldn't mind going to the library by yourself," Jessica suggested eagerly. She didn't think it was a big enough deal to warrant missing the football game.

"Gee, I don't know about that, Jessica." Winston's face grew as red as his ears. "You know I'm kind of . . . shy," he said with embarrassment. "People coming up and talking to me all day? That would be rough."

Jessica's mind was racing; she certainly didn't want to miss the football game. "Tell you what,

Winston. I'll just stay at the game until halftime. Then I'll come over to the library. You could even go home then if you want.''

Winston looked immensely relieved. ''That wouldn't be too bad. I think I could handle a half a day by myself.''

''All right, then that's what we'll do.''

''Deal.'' Winston stuck out his hand.

Jessica shook it. ''Deal.''

Because of her meeting, Jessica was late getting home. Elizabeth was already helping Mrs. Wakefield prepare dinner when Jessica came through the door looking grim.

''Hi, Jess. I didn't tell Mom,'' Elizabeth said gaily. ''I figured you'd want the honor.''

''Honor of what?'' Mrs. Wakefield looked up expectantly from the tomatoes she was slicing.

''It didn't happen,'' Jessica said dejectedly.

''Gee, I'm sorry, Jess.''

''What are you two talking about?'' Mrs. Wakefield asked.

Jessica explained her meeting with Mr. Siegal as tears welled up in her eyes.

Mrs. Wakefield gave her a big hug. ''Oh, Jessica, I know you're disappointed after you worked so hard, but it's a wonderful honor to be invited to exhibit in the library. I'm very proud of you.''

''You are?'' Jessica asked.

''And Daddy will be, too,'' her mother assured her. ''I only wish we could be there to see you.''

"You can't?" Jessica wailed.

"Daddy and I have tickets to a matinée that afternoon. I'm afraid it's too late to exchange the tickets."

"This is getting worse by the moment."

"I'll come, Jess," Elizabeth promised.

Jessica sniffed. "Will you? I'm taking the second shift."

"I'll come after the game," Elizabeth promised. "A whole crowd of kids should be there by then."

Jessica began to feel better. Maybe it wasn't the science fair, but it was something.

"I don't think I need any more help in here, girls. Why don't you get started on your homework?" Mrs. Wakefield suggested.

"All right," Elizabeth said, wiping her hands on a towel.

Jessica followed Elizabeth into the den. "Did you hear about Patrick?" Elizabeth asked. "His parents still won't let him join the band."

For a second, Jessica forgot about her own troubles. "I know. Can you believe it? Even after he proved to them that he could manage his studies and his practicing."

"I talked to him at lunch. He's really upset."

"Boy, I can't believe that they would be so mean," Jessica said, her eyes blazing.

Elizabeth was solemn. "Patrick was really hurt about the whole thing. He's furious with his parents. I've never seen him like this before, Jess. It was scary."

Jessica tried to ease her sister's mind. "He'll get over it, Lizzie. He really doesn't have a choice."

Elizabeth was waiting for Jessica to finish getting dressed when Patrick stopped by on Saturday morning.

"Hi, Patrick. Come on in," Elizabeth said.

Just then Jessica appeared at the bottom of the steps. She was wearing a bright red oversize shirt over her new white pants. Elizabeth was more casually attired in faded jeans and her freshly-washed green T-shirt.

"Aren't you a little dressed up for a football game, Jess?" Elizabeth asked.

"I want to look nice later when I go to the library."

"Oh, that's right. I forgot."

Patrick seemed not to have heard a word they said. "Today's the day I should have been playing with the band," he announced sadly.

"I know," Elizabeth said sympathetically. "But you're going to the game, aren't you?"

"No way." Patrick shook his head emphatically.

"Moping around isn't going to do you any good. You might as well come with us," Jessica reasoned.

"I'm not going to sit in the stands when I should be on the field," Patrick insisted.

Julie Porter and Ken Matthews appeared at the door. "Hi, everyone," Julie said. "We thought we'd walk over to the game with you."

"Bad luck about you not being in the band," Ken said.

"Yeah," Patrick muttered, obviously embarrassed that everyone knew about his problem.

"You know," Julie began hesitantly, "my mother might know someone who'd give you private lessons."

Patrick laughed bitterly. "If my folks won't let me join the band, I don't think they'll be willing to offer me private lessons."

Elizabeth hated to see Patrick with that hard, closed-up expression on his face. "Patrick," she began, "I know you think your parents are doing this out of pure meanness . . ."

"Of course they are," he interrupted.

"But there's got to be a reason." Julie finished Elizabeth's thought.

Angrily, Patrick rose to his feet. "I don't know why you're taking their side. I thought you were my friends."

"Hey, we are your friends," Ken said, putting a hand on Pat's shoulder.

"Everybody's got advice for me, but nobody understands how I feel. I'm sick and tired of people trying to run my life." His voice wobbled dangerously, and he turned and ran out of the Wakefields' house to hide his tears.

"Whew!" Ken exclaimed. "He's really upset."

"He's certainly not taking this very well," Julie said. "And I don't think we're helping him much."

Just then, the phone rang and as usual, Jessica was the first to answer it.

"Hello?"

"Jess, guess what?" Lila began talking without even a "hi" in return. "Bruce Patman is having a party after the football game, and all the Unicorns are invited."

"Really?" Jessica exclaimed.

"And the Wild Ones might be playing there."

"The Wild Ones? Wow!"

"Yeah, Bruce really thought they were great the night we saw them at the lake," Lila said.

This was great news. Even though Bruce hadn't really noticed her at the concert, this would be another chance to show him how special she was. Then she suddenly remembered Winston—and the library. She was supposed to be there all afternoon.

"Are you there, Jessica?" Lila spoke up.

Well, she'd just have to change her plans. There was no way she was going to miss a party at Bruce's. "Do we meet over at Bruce's house?" Jessica asked.

"Well, the Unicorns are all walking over together."

"I'll see you at the stadium, then. Save me a seat."

Jessica stood by the phone and glanced at her watch. Winston was already at the library. He'd be really upset if he knew she wasn't coming to relieve him. So rather than calling him, Jessica decided it would be best to simply not show up.

"Jessica." Mrs. Wakefield interrupted her thoughts. "Your dad and I are leaving. Good luck at the library."

Jessica stood still for a second. She wanted to tell her parents she wouldn't be attending, but before she could say a word, Mrs. Wakefield gave her a kiss and hurried out the door after her husband.

For a moment Jessica felt guilty. Her parents thought she was going to the library when she had no intention of going there. She calmed herself with the thought they would probably never know the difference and soon was convinced that it really didn't matter one way or the other.

The football game was an exciting match with first one team, then the other taking the lead. Jessica was in the midst of a cheering throng but her mind was on the exciting afternoon to come. Only when the band stepped out on the field did she think of Patrick. She glanced around to see if he had come to the game after all, but he was nowhere to be seen.

When Sweet Valley Middle School was assured a victory in the fourth quarter, Lila whispered to Jessica, "Why don't we start walking over to Bruce's? That way we can avoid the crowd."

"Good idea," Jessica said. Ellen Riteman, Kimberly Haver, and Janet Howell also gathered up their belongings. "I'm just going to say something to Elizabeth before I leave. I'll catch up to you."

She made her way to where Elizabeth and her friends were sitting. She had already told Elizabeth that she didn't have to go to the library exhibit but hadn't mentioned anything about the party. "Lizzie, I'm going to leave with the Unicorns," she said.

"All right. See you later," Elizabeth said, her eyes still on the field.

Jessica hurried off to join the Unicorns who laughed and whispered as they walked toward Bruce's house. Along the way, they passed the public library and Jessica felt a twinge of guilt. Winston was surely impatient for her to arrive, but she reasoned that she was actually doing him a favor. Winston was really too shy. Having people asking him a lot of questions about the exhibit would do him a world of good.

The Unicorns arrived at the Patmans' lavish home just a few moments after Bruce and some of his friends. Over the iron fence they could see Charlie Cashman doing a fake karate chop on big Jerry McAllister.

"The yard doesn't really look like it's set up for a party," Lila said as she peered over Jessica's shoulder.

"Maybe it's going to be inside," Kimberly suggested.

"It's too nice a day," observed Janet Howell, the president of the Unicorns.

The girls strolled through the tall wrought-iron gate and into the yard. Bruce and his friends barely looked up from their rough play. "Hey," Bruce finally said, when the girls were practically in front of them, "make yourselves comfortable."

Jessica and the other Unicorns looked around.

Although there were several deck and lounge chairs set up around the garden, there weren't enough for all of them. And soon, more kids streamed through the gate. The large crowd milled under the hot sun, accidentally stepping on flowers and waiting for the fun to start.

Jessica, who was eager to get Bruce's attention, went up to him and asked coyly, "Can I help you put out the food?"

Bruce looked blank. "What food?"

"Well, you invited all these kids over." Jessica gestured across the yard. "Didn't you expect to serve refreshments?"

"Not really," Bruce said. "I figured everyone would be stuffed from eating at the game."

"Oh," Jessica said, deflated. "You're not even having drinks?"

Bruce nodded. "Yeah, I told the housekeeper to buy some Cokes and stuff. Hey, Charlie," he called. "Help me haul out the drinks."

Charlie and Jerry followed Bruce into the house and reappeared, each carrying a couple of large bottles of cola. Bruce set them out on the patio table and twisted off the caps. Then he put out a stack of paper cups.

"Don't you even have ice?" Janet said with disgust.

Bruce shrugged. "Sure. In the house. Feel free to get some." He walked back to the lawn, picked up the football, and started tossing it around with a couple of the guys.

"Boy, what a drag this is," Ellen complained.

"I wouldn't even call it a party," Kimberly said. "And that was a rumor about the Wild Ones coming. There's not even going to be any music."

"That figures," Janet said.

Jessica felt worst of all. She could have been at the library, listening to people praise her project, instead of being stuck in the middle of a restless crowd. It was only four o'clock. Maybe if she left right now, she could still get to the library.

"I'm leaving," she told Ellen. "I've never been so bored."

"I don't blame you," Ellen replied.

Jessica looked over her shoulder to wave goodbye to Janet and Lila when she suddenly found herself headlong on the grass. She opened her eyes to see Jerry McAllister hovering over her. "Sorry, Jessica," he said. "I was going out for a pass."

A mortified Jessica looked up to see a crowd looking down at her. Then she heard Bruce's voice. "Hey, Wakefield, couldn't you watch where you were going?"

"Me?" Jessica sputtered, getting up with a little help from Jerry.

"Yeah. Heads up next time." He turned and began tossing the ball around again.

"Do you want to go inside to clean up?" Ellen whispered to her.

Jessica looked down in horror at her brand new outfit. It was covered with dirt. There was no way she could go to the library now. She scolded herself for wasting the afternoon for someone as selfish and ill-mannered as Bruce. If only she'd gone to the library where people would have appreciated her.

Furiously, she stomped off and headed home. "Lizzie," she called as soon as she opened the Wakefields' front door. "You'll never guess . . ." But her words died away when she saw Elizabeth's pale face leaning over the banister. "What's wrong?" she demanded.

"It's awful, Jess. Patrick's disappeared."

Seven

"All right, calm down, and tell us what the Morrises told you," Mr. Wakefield said. The twins' parents hadn't even parked the car in the driveway before the girls had come tumbling out of the house, talking at the same time.

Mrs. Wakefield had shepherded them inside, and sat them down in the living room. Now, Mr. Wakefield was trying to get a coherent story out of them.

"It was Liz who took the call," Jessica began.

Elizabeth nodded. "Mrs. Morris wanted to know if Patrick was at our house, and I told her he had been here earlier, but that he'd left before we went to the game. Then she asked if we had seen him there."

"And did you?" Mrs. Wakefield interjected.

Both girls shook their heads solemnly. "I looked around the stadium," Jessica said, "but I didn't see him anywhere."

"He wasn't there with the rest of the band?" Mr. Wakefield asked, confused. "He was so excited about making the band."

The girls hadn't told their parents about Patrick's troubles, but now they quickly blurted out all the details. Mr. and Mrs. Wakefield exchanged sober glances.

"Why don't you girls make a few phone calls, and see if any of your friends have seen Patrick," Mr. Wakefield suggested.

But before the twins could go to the phone, the doorbell rang. "Maybe that's Patrick," Jessica said, flying to the door. But when she opened it, there stood Winston, and he looked angry.

"What happened to you, Jessica?" Winston demanded.

Jessica looked nervously over her shoulder and saw her family listening with interest. Before Winston could continue, she quickly said, "Patrick's missing."

"What?"

Jessica told him everything she knew. "We're going to call around and see if anyone knows anything."

"Come in, Winston," Mrs. Wakefield said, "we have two telephone lines. Maybe you could help make some calls."

"All right," he agreed.

For the next hour, the twins and Winston managed to call most of their friends from school. Not one had seen Patrick.

"No luck," Jessica stated, coming back into the living room and flopping down on a chair.

"Now what do we do?" Elizabeth wanted to know.

Mr. and Mrs. Wakefield looked at each other helplessly. When the phone rang, Elizabeth ran to answer it. "Really?" she said. "You're sure of that? Thanks, Ken."

Elizabeth hung up the phone. "That was Ken Matthews returning my call. He's sure that he saw Patrick at the game, sitting off by a grove of trees far from the bleachers."

"I think we'd better call the Morrises and let them know," Mr. Wakefield said, heading toward the kitchen phone.

"I think I'd better go home. I really wasn't planning to stay this long," Winston announced. "Uh, Jessica, could you tell me . . . ?"

"I'll walk Winston to the door," Jessica said quickly, as she hustled him toward the front hall. She didn't want to be questioned about her whereabouts that afternoon, especially not in front of her parents.

Putting on her most innocent expression, Jessica started to explain, "Winston, I know you think I just left you hanging at the library . . ."

"Well, didn't you?" Winston broke in.

"I did it for your own good." Jessica looked up at him with wide blue-green eyes.

"My own good?" Winston cried. "What do you mean?"

Jessica nodded. "I know how shy you are, and I thought leaving you alone would be a good way to get you to talk to people."

"Come on, Jessica, you probably just had something better to do," Winston said accusingly.

Jessica didn't answer. Instead she asked, "Did you do all right with the visitors at the library?"

"Sure I did. A lot of people came up and talked to me."

"Well, then." Jessica lifted her hands. "It worked."

Winston drew himself up to his full height. "It still wasn't a very nice thing to do, Jessica. We were supposed to be partners." He gave her an angry look before slamming the door behind him.

Later that evening, when the Wakefields had finished dinner, Steven got up to clear the table. "There's a police car pulling up in our driveway!" he exclaimed, looking out the window.

The twins exchanged frightened looks. Could something have happened to Patrick?

Mr. Wakefield's voice was calm, but he looked unusually stern. "I'll go see what they want."

"Maybe they're coming to tell us Patrick has been found," Mrs. Wakefield said optimistically.

But when he reappeared, Mr. Wakefield didn't look relieved. "Could you all come into the living room?" he asked. "The police want to question us. Mr. and Mrs. Morris are with them."

Elizabeth felt sorry for the Morrises when she saw them standing in the Wakefield living room.

Mrs. Morris's eyes were red from crying, while Mr. Morris nervously clasped and unclasped his hands. They both looked exhausted.

Mr. Wakefield introduced his family to Officer Kirkland, a lanky man whose freckles made him look boyish. Still, it made Elizabeth uncomfortable to see a police officer with a gun in his holster right in the middle of her living room.

Officer Kirkland began questioning the Wakefields as soon as everyone sat down. He wanted to know whether Patrick had been upset about anything.

Elizabeth hesitated, but Jessica plunged right in with an answer. "Yes. He was very upset because he wasn't allowed to be in the school band."

Mrs. Morris looked down at the carpet, but Mr. Morris spoke up. "I know Patrick thought we were being cruel, but there were a lot of reasons we couldn't allow him to be in the band."

Officer Kirkland wrote something down in his notebook. "Anything else?"

Elizabeth saw Jessica looking at her. She knew her twin wanted her to speak up as well. Clearing her throat nervously, Elizabeth said, "Patrick was also unhappy that he couldn't go to the special concert the school sponsored last week."

"He told us his allowance had been cut and that he had to do tons of extra homework," Jessica chimed in.

Softly, Elizabeth said, "He felt his parents were being unreasonable."

"He thought they didn't love him," Jessica added.

Mrs. Morris's hand went to her throat. "Oh, no," she moaned.

Mr. Morris, too, seemed shaken by this accusation.

"Do you have any idea where Patrick could have gone?" Officer Kirkland asked the twins.

Both girls shook their heads.

"Are you conducting a search?" Mr. Wakefield wanted to know.

"Technically, we can't start searching until he's been missing for twenty-four hours," Officer Kirkland said regretfully. "But I want to get information gathered so that when that time is up, we can get right on it."

"What about an unofficial search?" Steven piped up.

"What do you mean?" the policeman wanted to know.

"I could get a few of my friends together," Steven said eagerly. "We could get started with the search."

Officer Kirkland walked to the window and peered out. "I wouldn't recommend you begin until tomorrow morning. I see no harm in you trying it then."

"I'll go with you, Steve," Mr. Wakefield said. "We'll get started first thing in the morning."

It was a long, restless night for Elizabeth. She couldn't forget the look of worry on Mrs. Morris's face, nor the fact that Patrick's mother had laid her hand on Elizabeth's arm. "Thank you for being my son's friend," she'd said quietly.

When she heard Jessica shuffling in the bathroom the two of them shared, Elizabeth called to her through the door, "Jess, would you come in?"

Jessica came in rubbing her eyes. "It's the middle of the night, Liz."

"I know, but I can't sleep." She slid over so Jessica would have room to sit on the edge of her bed.

"I'm sure Patrick's all right," Jessica said. "You have to admit, he had so many reasons to run away."

"Jess, it's not safe to be out roaming the streets at night. He could be in danger."

"Maybe he found a place to stay."

Elizabeth shook her head. "I hope so. But I keep thinking he's sleeping in a park or in a doorway somewhere."

Jessica got under the covers, pulled Elizabeth's blanket up to her chin, and said, "Steven called some of his friends and they're going to search for Patrick as soon as it's light. Don't worry, they'll find him."

"He could have hitched a ride with a stranger," Elizabeth continued, worried. "He could be in trouble somewhere."

Jessica's response was a soft snore. Elizabeth tried to roll over, but room was tight now that Jessica was sharing her twin bed. She tossed and turned for what seemed like forever, then finally fell asleep, dreaming about Patrick huddled in a doorway, shivering.

Eight

◇

Elizabeth had only been asleep a couple of hours when she heard her father and Steven up and about. Slipping out of bed, she grabbed her robe and ran downstairs. Mr. Wakefield and Steven were dressed and ready to go.

"Can I come, too?" Elizabeth pleaded. "It'll just take me a minute to get ready."

"Honey, we decided last night it would be better if Steven and his friends searched through the forest preserve. You and Jessica can try some of the spots closer to home."

"But, Dad—"

"No buts. I'm sure this will be the most efficient way to do things." Mr. Wakefield put his arm around Elizabeth and squeezed her shoulder.

"All right," Elizabeth gave in. "I'll wake Jessica and we'll search around the neighborhood together."

"Don't worry, kiddo," Steven said. "Patrick will turn up. Let's go, Dad."

Deciding some breakfast might help the empty feeling inside her, Elizabeth poured cereal and milk into a bowl. Before she started eating, she was startled by a sound on the back porch. It was so early—not even seven—that Elizabeth couldn't imagine who would want to visit at this hour.

Thinking it might be Patrick, Elizabeth ran to the door, but no one was there. She looked around carefully before noticing the tip of a white envelope stuck in the outer door frame. She pulled it out and examined it. There was no name on it, so Elizabeth tore it open. Inside was a piece of paper with crude writing on it.

WE HAVE PATRICK. STOP LOOKING FOR HIM.
IF YOU DON'T IT COULD BE VERY BAD
FOR HIM.

Elizabeth stood on the porch for a moment, clutching the note. Then she ran back inside and up the stairs to her bedroom.

"Wake up, Jess," Elizabeth said, shaking her sister.

"Wha-at?" Jessica tried to roll over but Elizabeth wouldn't let her. She shoved the note into her hand. "Read this."

Reluctantly Jessica read the short note and bolted upright. "Does this mean Patrick's been kidnapped?" she cried.

"It must."

"Have you told Mom or Dad yet?" Jessica wanted to know. Now she was wide awake.

"Dad and Steven have already left." With a catch in her throat, Elizabeth added, "I didn't want to tell Mom alone."

Jessica rolled out of bed, and together the girls hurried to their mother's room.

Mrs. Wakefield was just finishing dressing, when she saw the wide-eyed twins standing in the doorway. "What's wrong?" she asked with concern.

"We think Patrick's been kidnapped," Jessica said, as Elizabeth handed her mother the note.

"I'm going to call the police," Mrs. Wakefield said, hurrying to the phone.

After a brief conversation with the police department, Mrs. Wakefield turned to her daughters. "Get dressed, girls. Officer Kirkland will be here soon. I'm sure he'll want to talk to you."

By the time the policeman arrived, the girls were dressed and anxiously pacing the length of the living room. After Officer Kirkland scanned the note, and asked Elizabeth to tell him how she had found it, he said, "We'll check this out, but I have a feeling this is a fake."

"A fake?" Elizabeth exclaimed.

"Why do you think that?" Mrs. Wakefield asked more calmly.

"Kidnappers usually ask for a ransom. There's nothing about that here. Besides, why didn't the person deliver the note to the Morrises?"

Mrs. Wakefield looked relieved. "So, you're assuming it could be some sort of a cruel joke?"

"Perhaps. I don't want to say much more until I have a chance to investigate, but I certainly would say this is not from professional kidnappers."

Telling them he would call the Morrises and get back to them as soon as he knew anything more, Officer Kirkland took the note and said he'd examine it for fingerprints down at the stationhouse.

It was still early and the morning stretched on endlessly for Elizabeth and Jessica. "Why don't you girls go out and see some friends?" Mrs. Wakefield suggested. "There's not much more you can do sitting at home."

"Daddy did want us to check around the neighborhood," Elizabeth remembered.

"That's an excellent idea," Mrs. Wakefield said heartily. "Maybe by the time you get back your father and Steven will be here."

"OK, Mom, we'll see you later. Let's go, Jess." Elizabeth grabbed a sweater from the hall closet and then the girls walked out to the street. To their surprise, they spotted Winston approaching their house.

Oh, no, Jessica thought to herself. *I hope he's not going to start bugging me about the library exhibit again.*

But, when Winston came up to them, he blurted out some unexpected news. "I know where Patrick is."

"What?" Elizabeth exclaimed.

"Where?" Jessica demanded.

Winston pulled them down the street, farther away from their home, so they wouldn't be overheard. "He's in my basement."

Elizabeth couldn't have been more shocked if Winston had told them Patrick was on the moon. "What in the world is he doing there?"

They settled themselves on a bench so Winston could explain the whole thing. "I was so exhausted from the library exhibit yesterday afternoon that I just wanted to go to bed early last night. My parents were out for the evening, and I was in my room reading when I heard someone throwing stones at the window."

"Patrick?" Elizabeth said, gasping.

Winston nodded. "I opened the window and told him to come around the back so no one would see him."

"Then what happened?" Jessica asked impatiently.

"He told me he couldn't stand living at home anymore and was running away. But he didn't have much money with him, and he asked if I could put him up for the night."

Elizabeth frowned. "Didn't you try to get him to go home? His parents are frantic."

"The police were over at our house last night," Jessica told Winston. "They're starting a search."

"Patrick knows that. He saw them drive up. He was actually going to ask you to let him sleep in the shed where he practiced the saxophone. But when he saw the police, he came to me instead."

Suddenly, a thought occurred to Elizabeth. "Winston, did you have anything to do with a note that was delivered to our house this morning?"

Winston wiped his brow. "Yeah."

"You were the one who put it in our doorway?" Jessica screeched.

"It was a mistake, I know," Winston said, his voice full of remorse. "Patrick slept in our basement, and this morning, when I went down to check on him, he had already written it. He didn't want to risk being seen, so he begged me to bring it over to your house."

"Couldn't you have said no?" Elizabeth demanded. "Mr. and Mrs. Morris are going to be scared to death when they read that letter. They'll think a kidnapper has their son."

"I know," Winston moaned. "But Pat said he'd leave and never come back if I didn't do it."

"Then I think you did the right thing," Jessica said, surprised to hear herself standing up for Winston.

Winston was surprised, too. "You do?"

"Well, you bought some time, didn't you?"

"That's right." Winston was happy that someone understood his motives. "I figured if Patrick left my house we might never see him again. I knew the note was going to cause all kinds of problems, but that seemed like a better solution than having him take off."

"You could be right," Elizabeth admitted. "It

would have been terrible if he had just disappeared. And awfully dangerous, too."

Jessica got up, smoothing the creases from her blue poplin shorts. "We have to go see him."

"That's what I was hoping you'd say," Winston admitted, relieved. "My parents are at my grandmother's house, but they'll be back by noon. We haven't got much time."

"Then what are we waiting for," Jessica said decisively. She set a quick pace as they hurried over to Winston's house.

Winston led the girls down to the basement room that his father had fixed up as a home office. A couch with a blanket thrown over it had obviously been Patrick's bed last night. But Patrick was nowhere to be seen.

"You don't think he left, do you?" Elizabeth asked.

Winston looked perplexed until he heard the sound of the shower coming from the basement bathroom. "He must be washing up. He was pretty dirty after hiding out all day."

Winston went to check on Patrick and a moment later the two of them were back. Patrick, his hair still wet, was wearing his jeans and a large shirt of Winston's. "Hi, guys."

"I don't know whether to kiss you or kill you!" Elizabeth admitted.

"Hey, don't do either one." Patrick cracked a smile.

Jessica flopped down on the couch. "Well, I

have to congratulate you, Patrick. Even if you did worry us, you certainly got your parents' attention."

"I didn't exactly do it to get their attention," Patrick said, scuffing his bare foot against the linoleum floor.

"Then why did you do it?" Elizabeth asked.

Patrick's voice hardened. "Because it's pretty obvious my parents don't like me. I just want to get away from them and all their stupid rules."

"Oh, Pat, you should have seen them last night," Elizabeth said. "They were so worried."

"Good!" Patrick said, his voice firm.

Elizabeth was appalled. Was this the same sweet Patrick Morris she knew so well?

"I think Patrick's parents deserve to be punished," Jessica said.

Elizabeth looked at Jessica in horror. "How can you say that, Jess? Patrick's got to go home."

"No way." Patrick shook his head.

"Patrick's right. He shouldn't go home," Jessica agreed. "At least not until he gets some concessions from his parents."

"What kind of concessions?" Winston asked worriedly.

"Only one hour of homework a night," Jessica said, warming to her subject. "And a later curfew, on weekends at least."

Patrick interrupted her. "I don't want any concessions. I just want to leave."

"Be practical, Pat," Elizabeth said, trying to sound

reasonable. "You don't have any money. Where will you go?"

"Winston said he would lend me some money." Patrick turned to look at Winston who was staring miserably at the wall. "You said you had at least twenty dollars saved."

"I did. I mean I do, but twenty dollars isn't going to get you very far."

"It certainly isn't," Elizabeth said firmly.

"Well, it might get you as far as Pinecrest," Jessica mused.

"Jessica, will you be quiet!"

"Hey," Patrick said. "This is my life, remember? And I'm not going back."

Winston sat down heavily on the couch and ran his fingers through his hair. "Patrick, my parents will be home any minute now. My dad might come down to the basement to do some work. I don't see how you can stay."

"I told you I'm leaving," Patrick replied. "I'll go right now, if you give me the twenty dollars."

Winston looked helplessly at Elizabeth, but she didn't know what to say either.

Finally, Jessica spoke up. "Patrick doesn't have to go. He can hang around the mall—nobody would notice an extra kid there—or he can go to the library and read all day. Tonight he can come back here, or stay in our shed. It wouldn't be any trouble to leave the door open, right, Liz?"

There was a moment of silence as everyone looked at Elizabeth. "No, that is *not* right. Patrick, you have to come with us right now. Your parents are worried to death. No matter how angry you are, I think you have to go home and talk to your mom and dad."

"I haven't decided what I'll do next, but I know I'm *not* going home." Then he stared at Elizabeth. "You won't tell my parents where I am, will you? If you do, I'll never forgive you."

Patrick's words hung in the air like icicles. Elizabeth felt torn and confused, but at last she replied. "All right, if that's what you want, I won't tell."

Nine

The twins walked home in silence. When they opened the front door, they found their parents, Steven, and the Morrises sitting in the kitchen, each one looking more upset than the next.

The saddest-looking of all were Mr. and Mrs. Morris. Mrs. Morris was wearing the same clothing she had had on the day before. Her eyes were puffy and red-rimmed. Mr. Morris was unshaven, and there were dark circles under his eyes. It was obvious both of them had gotten almost no sleep.

"Any news?" Mrs. Wakefield asked her daughters, as she refilled Mr. Morris's cup with coffee.

Yes! Elizabeth wanted to shout, but she felt a pressure in her side where Jessica was poking her.

Mr. Wakefield took the twins' silence for a no. "We didn't have much luck either," he said.

"There is one piece of good news," Mr. Morris added, trying to look optimistic. "That note you received wasn't from kidnappers. The police think it was just some kids playing a joke."

"That's good," Jessica said cheerfully. Elizabeth marveled at her sister's acting ability.

"Well, we've kept you all long enough," Mr. Morris said, taking one final sip of coffee.

"The younger boys are home with my sister," Mrs. Morris explained. "They're very upset. I don't want to leave them for too long."

Mr. Morris patted his wife's hand. "I just don't know how much longer any of us can go on like this."

"It's the uncertainty that's killing me," Mrs. Morris said, her eyes filling with tears.

That did it! Elizabeth couldn't remain silent any longer. Even if Patrick never spoke to her again, she simply couldn't continue to watch Mr. and Mrs. Morris suffering.

Before Jessica could do anything to stop her, Elizabeth blurted out her news. "Patrick's over at Winston Egbert's house."

"What?" Her father sprang up. "Why didn't you tell us as soon as you walked in?"

Elizabeth looked for help in Jessica's direction, but her sister was studying the ceiling. "He begged us not to tell," Elizabeth said miserably.

"Oh, Elizabeth," Mrs. Wakefield said, sounding very disappointed.

"It's OK, Elizabeth. As long as he's all right." Mr. Morris got up and put his arms around both girls' shoulders. "It was hard to do that, I know, but telling us was the right thing. We have a lot to talk about with Patrick—and a lot to explain to him."

Mrs. Morris joined her husband. "How do we get to Winston's house?"

"I'd like to go over, too," Mr. Wakefield said. "You can follow us."

The whole Wakefield family piled into the van and the Morrises climbed into their car. As they were driving to Winston's, Mrs. Wakefield turned to her daughters in the back. "I still don't understand, girls. How could you not tell us about Patrick right away? You know how frantic everyone's been."

"The two of you seemed as upset as everyone else," Mr. Wakefield added.

"We were," Elizabeth burst out. "We didn't know where Patrick was until this morning."

Jessica stared out the window. "Patrick's parents are so mean. It's no wonder he ran away."

Mr. Wakefield looked at Jessica in the rearview mirror. "I know that's how you feel—and how Patrick feels—but we don't know their side of the story, Jessica. Things aren't always what they seem."

Before Mr. Wakefield could say any more, they arrived at Winston's house. As they got out, Winston came running out of the house. From the frightened look on his face, the twins knew immediately that something was wrong.

"I was just calling you," Winston said, out of breath. "Patrick's run away again. He knew you'd break down and tell, Elizabeth, and he said he was leaving before you came back with the police—or his parents." He glanced nervously at Mr. and Mrs. Morris.

"Do you know where he's gone?" Mr. Morris demanded.

Winston nodded. "I followed him. He ran into that abandoned church on Somerset Street."

"Oh, no!" Mr. Morris covered his face with his hands. "My construction crew examined that building recently. It's been condemned by the city. It's not safe for anyone to be inside that church."

"What shall we do?" Mrs. Morris cried.

"Let's get over there. Maybe we can talk him into coming out."

"Winston, call the police—and the fire department. We might need their equipment," Mr. Wakefield ordered.

As quickly as possible, the Wakefields and Mr. and Mrs. Morris drove to Somerset Street. Elizabeth knew the church. At one time it had been a beautiful building of stucco and wood with intricate stained-glass windows. But the congregation had long ago purchased a larger building and the church had stood empty for years, slowly falling into disrepair.

Now, as Elizabeth jumped out of the van, she could see what terrible condition the building was in. The sidewalk around it was littered with pieces of stucco that had fallen from the decaying building, and the lovely glass was now full of jagged holes. Running to the doorway of the church, she peeked inside and saw a large entry hall with rotting wood and fallen ceilings. Beyond it was a room full of rubble that must have been used for church services. The church reminded her of condemned buildings she had seen on the news.

"Elizabeth, stay away from there," her father yelled.

Shaking, she drew back. "It's horrible in there," Elizabeth whispered to her twin. "The whole thing looks like it could fall down any second."

Mr. Morris was wasting no time finding out if Patrick was inside. "Pat," he called from the middle of the empty street. "Are you in there, son?"

His wife joined in. "Honey, please, let us know if you're OK."

There was a silence that seemed to last forever, then high up, in a third-story window, Patrick's face appeared.

"Pat, are you all right?" Steven shouted.

Patrick nodded. Then he cupped his hands and yelled down. "I'm not coming out."

"Please, Patrick," Mrs. Morris said, trying to contain her tears.

"Patrick, listen to me. This building's not safe. You could fall through the floor any minute. Just stay put. Someone will be here to rescue you soon."

Instead of being frightened, Patrick grew angry. "I don't want anyone to rescue me. I got up here all right, and I'll get out all right—when I'm ready. When all of you go away."

Mr. Morris kept his voice calm. "We just want to talk to you, Pat. I know you're angry, and maybe you have a right to be, but I promise we can get things worked out once you're safely out of there."

For a moment Patrick looked as if he was going to heed his father's advice. He stood still as a stone, not moving from the window. Then, the sound of a fire-engine siren filled the air. A police car followed with its own distinctive whine. Patrick jerked his head in the direction of the noise, looking frightened.

"Don't move," Mr. Morris yelled, but Patrick leapt away from the window. The next sound everyone heard was a loud, horrible crash!

"Patrick," Mrs. Morris cried, as her husband sprang toward the entrance to the church.

"No, you don't, buddy." A fireman appeared from out of nowhere. He grabbed Mr. Morris's arms and held him back.

"But that's my son," Mr. Morris said in a tight voice, struggling out of the fireman's grip.

"Look." The fireman pointed toward the window where a crew was cranking up an extension ladder to the third floor. "We'll get there faster than you can."

Mrs. Morris was sobbing loudly when Winston ran up and joined the twins. "I hope he's all right," Jessica said, her voice quivering.

After what seemed like forever, the firemen secured their ladder against the side of the building and entered the church through the third-story window.

"They'll be out with him in no time," Mrs. Wakefield said, trying to sound cheerful. But almost as soon as they got into the building, they came back out—alone.

"Where is he?" Mrs. Morris moaned.

The firemen quickly conferred with their chief upon exiting the building. Then the gray-haired chief hurried over to talk to them.

"I'm Captain Williams," he said. "At the moment the boy is fine, but he has fallen through some rotting wood and he's trapped between floors."

Mrs. Morris gasped and closed her eyes.

"What are you going to do to get him out?" Mr. Morris demanded.

"I've radioed for some extra equipment. I'll send one of my men to the window to keep him calm until help arrives."

"We can't wait that long," Mr. Morris said, springing forward.

"No, please, don't go in there," the fire chief shouted as Mr. Morris disappeared into the debris-strewn building. Ignoring the pleas of Captain Williams, Mr. Morris made his way toward a metal stairway along the east side of the building that was still in reasonable shape. Stepping carefully but quickly, he climbed up, all the while yelling words of encouragement to his son. "It's all right, Patrick. Don't worry. I'm on my way."

When Mr. Morris reached the third floor, he could see his terrified son in the center of the huge room, stuck in a small hole in the decaying wooden floor. Patrick was only visible from the waist up, his hands clutching the legs of an old desk that was within reach.

"Dad!" Patrick screamed, when he caught sight

of his father. "It'll be all right, Patrick." Mr. Morris inched his way from the metal stairway toward one of the windows on the adjoining wall. He saw one of the firemen on a ladder leaning against the window ledge. "Get out of there," the fireman implored. "Wait until the equipment arrives."

"I have to help my son. I can't wait another second. And I need your help, too. Throw me some rope," Mr. Morris commanded.

The fireman shook his head. "It'll never work," he said. Suddenly, a sharp crack caused both men to turn in Patrick's direction. More of the floor had given in. The hole was widening, and Patrick, clutching the desk even tighter to maintain his position, let out a horrifying scream.

"Pat!" Mr. Morris yelled. He started to run toward Patrick, but his weight made the whole floor shudder. He turned back toward the window. The fireman threw him a length of rope, tying one end to the ladder he was standing on.

With agonizingly slow movements, Mr. Morris crawled toward Patrick. There were groans and creaks every step of the way, but finally he was close enough to get the rope to Patrick.

He made a lasso with his end, then yelled to the fireman, "I'm going to lower him down. Have a net waiting."

"Dad, I'm sorry," Patrick said, his face streaked with tears.

"Don't think about that now. Just listen to me carefully and follow my instructions." Forcing calm into his voice, he explained to Patrick what needed to be done. "I can't get much closer without the floor cracking wide open. I'm going to toss this lasso to you. Try to hook it around your waist, and I'll lower you down."

He tossed the rope to Patrick, who took it with one shaking hand while he held on to the desk leg with the other. After two tries, Patrick managed to secure the rope around his waist. "Tight on your end?" Mr. Morris called to the fireman.

"Solid," he called back.

"Patrick, that hole is big enough for you to slip through," Mr. Morris said with urgency in his voice. "I'm going to lower you down. When you get close enough to the net, wiggle out of the rope and jump."

"No, Dad. I don't think I can do it."

"You can, Patrick. I know you can. You'll be very close to the net. The firemen might even be able to grab you."

Patrick and Mr. Morris looked at each other. Both had tears in their eyes.

"OK, Dad, I'll try," Patrick cried. "Here goes." He let go of the desk.

Mr. Morris began letting out the rope. In a few seconds, Patrick had disappeared down the hole. All the while, Mr. Morris kept up his encouragement. "You can do it, son. You're a brave boy. It won't be long now."

At last he heard shouts from the firemen below. "We've got him," they yelled.

"Thank God," Mr. Morris breathed. But there

was no time to waste. Now he had to get himself out of the rotting church.

"Try to get over here to the window," the fireman on the ladder called.

Mr. Morris began to tread softly back toward the window, but he had gone only a few steps when the floor began to give way. Standing frozen, he realized there was no way the floor would take the weight of his frame. Looking around desperately, his eye caught the metal stairway on the adjoining wall. The floor in that direction looked a little more sturdy. Maybe, just maybe, he could make it back over there.

"Be careful," the fireman called, sensing his intention.

Mr. Morris nodded grimly, his eyes focused on his goal. With the utmost care, he moved toward the staircase. Pieces of debris from the ceiling were falling around him, and the dust that had been stirred up from below made him cough.

Finally he caught hold of the rusty metal railing. For a moment, he just leaned against it to steady himself. Then he began to climb down the rickety stairs.

"There he is!" shouted Patrick when his father's form was visible on the last steps of the staircase.

Mr. Morris heard his voice and waved. He picked his way through the rubble-strewn floor, and once in the bright sunlight, he ran toward Patrick.

"Are you all right?" He gripped Patrick in his arms.

"I'm fine," Patrick sobbed.

Mr. Morris took a step back, so he could look Patrick over carefully. He touched a bruise starting to form on his son's forehead. "You're OK, son."

"Thanks to you, Dad," Patrick said, swallowing hard. Then he buried himself in his father's embrace.

Ten

◇

It took several minutes for everyone to catch their breath. Mrs. Morris kissed Patrick over and over until he finally squirmed away, and everyone congratulated Mr. Morris on his bravery.

"You're a very lucky young man, Patrick," the police chief said, coming up to the group. He shook Mr. Morris's hand. "And you, sir, have a lot to be proud of today."

"He certainly does." His wife smiled at him.

Mr. Morris and Patrick then recounted their hair-raising experience. "I couldn't believe it when Dad said I had to be lowered down that hole." Patrick shuddered. "I never thought I could do it."

"Was jumping into the net scary?" Winston demanded.

"It wasn't too bad. I didn't have too far to go."

"Boy," Steven joked, "between being lassoed and that net, you're ready to join a circus."

"No. I'd say he's ready to go home and have a nice hot cup of tea," Mrs. Morris said firmly, provoking laughter.

"Wow, this was exciting," Jessica said, her eyes sparkling. "Everyone's going to be talking about it tomorrow!"

Suddenly Patrick looked very, very tired. "It was *too* exciting." He turned to Elizabeth. "You told my parents where I was, didn't you?"

She nodded.

"I knew you would." Patrick gave her a small smile. "And, Elizabeth?"

"What?"

"I'm really glad you did."

Elizabeth knew this was Patrick's way of apologizing. "Thanks, Pat. I'm glad I did, too."

Finally, Mr. Wakefield said, "I think we should all be getting home. I know the Morrises have a lot to talk about."

Mr. Morris looked at Patrick. "You're right. There's plenty to sort out."

On their drive home, the Morris family was silent, each person lost in thought. Once they arrived home, Patrick was greeted joyfully by his brothers and his aunt. Then he and his parents sat down at the dining room table.

"Dad," Patrick began, "I'm really sorry. Going into that building was such a stupid thing to do." He paused for a few seconds. "So was running away, I guess."

"I hope you've learned that running away never solves anything," Mr. Morris said soberly.

"Maybe it doesn't, but I just didn't know how else to let you know I was angry, and hurt."

"We know you were, Patrick," his mother said soothingly. She reached over and patted his hand. "I think your father and I were both wrong not to tell you what was going on, and why we were making all those new rules."

"What was going on, Mom? Can you tell me now?"

Mrs. Morris looked at her husband, who cleared his throat. "The fact of the matter is, Patrick, I lost my job."

"You did?" Patrick couldn't have been more surprised. "But you were always gone during the day. Except that once," he remembered.

"I was looking for a new job," Mr. Morris replied with a sigh.

"And he never wanted you to know he wasn't working," Mrs. Morris added.

"Why, Dad?" Patrick asked. "I would have understood."

Mr. Morris looked surprised. "I guess I underestimated you, Patrick. I just didn't want you to worry."

"I was more worried when I couldn't figure out what was going on."

"We understand that now," Mrs. Morris said gravely, "but at the time we were trying to spare you all the heartache, all the worry . . ." Her voice trailed off.

Grabbing his pipe from his pocket, Mr. Morris filled the bowl with tobacco. "And that's why we cracked down on your studies. You've got to get good grades so you can go to college and have a profession or build your own business."

"Your father wants a more secure future for you than he's had," Mrs. Morris explained.

Mr. Morris puffed nervously on his pipe. "The worst part, Pat, was having you think we were mean and uncaring. When you wanted to join the band, we said no because we knew we couldn't afford the cost of lessons and the instrument." Mr. Morris shook his head.

"But it wouldn't have been expensive," Patrick declared.

"We priced a saxophone," his mother informed him. "They cost a small fortune."

"To buy. But the school will loan one to me for free. All I have to pay for is the mouthpiece and the reeds."

Mrs. Morris looked surprised. "We had no idea the school was so well-equipped," she said. "But lessons are still quite expensive, Patrick."

"I wouldn't have to have private lessons for now. Ms. McDonald would teach me everything I need to know."

Mr. Morris sadly rubbed the bowl of his pipe. "I guess there's plenty we didn't realize," he said. "We could have avoided all this trouble if we'd just been more honest with you. We should have talked more."

"Yeah," Patrick said soberly. "I was pretty angry."

"We realize that now, Patrick. But try to understand. Your father just couldn't bear for you to know he was out of work."

Patrick turned to his father eagerly. "I can help you, Dad. I'll get a paper route or something."

His father smiled at him warmly. "Thank you for offering, Patrick, but that isn't going to be necessary. I got a job as a foreman on another construction crew. It'll mean traveling a little more every day, but it'll be worth it. Besides, you'll be busy with all your schoolwork and band practice."

Patrick's face lit up. He stood up, ran over to his father, and threw his arms around him.

On the patio of the Wakefield house, another family discussion was under way. Mr. and Mrs. Wakefield were still upset that the girls hadn't come to them immediately upon knowing that Patrick was hiding at Winston's house.

"Are you going to punish us?" Jessica asked, unhappily.

"What do *you* think we should do?" Mrs. Wakefield replied, sipping a glass of ice tea.

"Well, I don't think we should be punished," Jessica put in.

"Why not?" Mr. Wakefield asked.

"We've been punished enough."

Her father began stoking up the barbecue grill. "How do you figure that?"

"First we were worried to death," Jessica explained. "And then we had to decide whether to break a friend's confidence or save his life," she added dramatically.

Elizabeth rolled her eyes. Leave it to Jessica to make it sound as though they hadn't done anything wrong.

"I am tempted to let this go by," Mrs. Wakefield said. "This has been very difficult for all of us."

"Your mother is right, girls. Let's put this episode in the past."

The twins exchanged relieved glances.

Steven, who had been inside, came wandering out to the patio with the Sunday edition of the *Sweet Valley Times* in his hand. "Hey, Jess, I thought you said you were at that science exhibit at the library."

Jessica gulped. "Uh, so?"

"Well, there's an article about the exhibit. And a picture of Winston Egbert and his mold." He handed the paper to Jessica. "It also says his partner, Jessica Wakefield, was not present."

Jessica could feel all eyes upon her as she read the article. She couldn't believe that Winston hadn't told her it was going to appear.

"Well, Jessica," Mr. Wakefield said sternly. "Why weren't you there?"

Jessica knew she was in trouble. Hanging her head, she said, "I didn't go, but it was for a good reason." Quickly, she tried to organize her thoughts. "It was for Winston's sake," she said, using the same argument on her parents that she had used on Winston. "He was terrified of speaking to strangers," she explained. "I knew that if I went to the library, he'd make me do all the talking. So I said I'd relieve him at halftime, and he agreed to that. Then I decided the best thing for Winston would be to spend the whole day by himself. And even though my picture isn't in the newspaper, I'm sure it was worth it!" A wide-eyed Jessica finished her explanation on a dramatic note.

Mrs. Wakefield looked at her skeptically. "More serious decision-making, Jessica?"

"Well, I hadn't promised Winston I'd go."

"How did Winston feel about your great sacrifice?" her father wanted to know.

"We really haven't had a chance to talk about it, with Patrick running away and all."

"I suggest that you do talk about it," Mr. Wakefield said dryly. "Winston may not be too pleased with you."

"I think you owe Winston an apology. I want your promise that you'll do that," her mother insisted.

"All right," Jessica agreed instantly. Was she going to be lucky enough to get off without a punishment twice in one day?

Mr. Wakefield put some steaks on the barbecue. "I suppose not getting your picture in the paper is punishment enough." There was a hint of a smile forming on his lips. He didn't quite sound convinced of Jessica's story, but she knew when to leave "well enough" alone. This was almost too good to be true.

"Thanks, Dad," Jessica said, relieved. "I'm going to phone Lila and tell her what happened today.

She'll never believe it," she called as she ran into the house.

Elizabeth closed her eyes and turned her face toward the sun. She didn't know the whole story, but she knew Jessica. There was more to this puzzle than Jessica wanting to help Winston overcome his shyness.

On Monday morning the twins arrived at school to find Patrick the center of attention. The story of his dramatic rescue had appeared in the papers and now there was a crowd of people around him wanting to hear all the details. Jessica decided to wander over and get her share of the glory, when she was waylaid by Winston.

"Well, are you ready to explain?" Winston said boldly.

"All right," Jessica said, sighing. "I apologize for leaving you hanging."

"You do?"

"Yes." Jessica didn't mention she was fulfilling a promise to her parents. "And even though leaving you alone in the library got you over your shyness, I'm not asking for any thanks."

"Oh, Jessica." Winston groaned.

"Well, look who's here, if it isn't 'Fall-down-and-go-boom Wakefield.' "

Jessica whirled around at the sound of Bruce Patman's voice. He was standing behind her, Jerry McAllister at his side. "I'll have to check and see if you left a hole in the ground, Jess," Bruce continued, with a laugh.

Jessica was so embarrassed she wanted to die. She couldn't think of a thing to say in response.

"Hey, Patman, if I recall correctly, you're not the most graceful guy in the world. Didn't they call you Four Feet a couple of years ago, because you kept tripping in gym?" Winston asked.

Bruce glared at Winston, but before he could answer, Jerry let out a huge laugh. "Four Feet. I'd forgotten about that."

"Well, forget it again," Bruce snapped. "Come on, let's get out of here." The boys took off, with Jerry still laughing.

Jessica looked at Winston with new respect. "Thanks for sticking up for me, Winston."

"Oh, don't mention it." His ears turned bright red.

Jessica could hardly believe it. She had always thought Winston was a real nerd, but in the last couple of weeks she had almost grown to like him. She looked around to make sure none of the Unicorns were nearby. "You know, Winston, you're all right," she whispered.

"I am?"

Jessica smiled. "But don't tell anyone I told you so."

"So, did you apologize to Winston?" Elizabeth asked as the twins walked home from school.

Jessica waved her hand. "All taken care of."

"That's good," Elizabeth said approvingly.

"Now that all this stuff with Patrick is over, I

want to have some fun. Maybe we could organize an overnight trip with some of our friends."

"I don't think Mom and Dad will let us go away without an adult."

"You know, Liz, I don't see why they don't think we're old enough to do anything on our own. They really treat us like babies sometimes," Jessica huffed.

"Well, I guess we'll just have to prove to them that we're responsible," Elizabeth replied.

"You're right, Liz. Now all we need is a plan. Just leave it to me."

What exciting scheme does Jessica have in mind? Find out in Sweet Valley Twins #27, **TEAMWORK.**

ANNOUNCING
THE

APRIL FOOLS' DAY
CONTEST

Just send us a description of your favorite prank or practical joke (be nice!). If yours is judged the most creative of the bunch, you could win one of these great prizes:

(1) GRAND PRIZE – The entry that makes us laugh the hardest will be published in Bantam's SNEAK PEEKS™ and LOVELETTERS newsletters. These newsletters get mailed to about 30,000 girls all over the world!

The grand prize winner and

(5) SECOND PRIZE – winning creative pranksters will receive an autographed copy of *APRIL FOOL!*, SWEET VALLEY TWINS #28, created by Francine Pascal, an autographed photo of Francine Pascal, and a SWEET VALLEY T-shirt.

SO WHAT ARE YOU WAITING FOR? Send your name, address, age and a description of your favorite prank to:

> BANTAM BOOKS
> YOUNG READERS MARKETING DEPT. A.F.
> 666 FIFTH AVE
> NEW YORK, NY 10103

Entries must be postmarked and received by March 15, 1989. Be sure to read the Official Rules on the next page!!

GOOD LUCK, and may the best
mischief-maker win!!!

ENTER THE
SWEET VALLEY TWINS™
APRIL FOOLS' DAY CONTEST

OFFICIAL RULES:

1) *No Purchase Is Necessary.* Enter by handprinting your name, address, age and telephone number on a plain 3″ x 5″ card, along with your description of an April Fools' prank, and send the card to:

> YOUNG READERS MARKETING, DEPT. AF
> Bantam Books
> 666 Fifth Avenue
> New York, New York 10103

2) *Prizes*

1 Grand Prize. The Grand Prize winner will have his or her contest submission published in Bantam's SNEAK PEEKS™ and LOVELETTERS direct mail promotional newsletters and will receive a copy of the April 1989 SWEET VALLEY TWINS™ publication, *APRIL FOOL!*, autographed by Francine Pascal, the creator of the SWEET VALLEY TWINS™ series, an autographed photograph of Francine Pascal, plus a SWEET VALLEY HIGH® T-shirt (approximate retail value: $20.00).

5 (Five) Second Prizes: Each Second Prize winner will receive a copy of the April 1989 SWEET VALLEY TWINS™ publication, *APRIL FOOL!*, autographed by Francine Pascal, the creator of the SWEET VALLEY TWINS™ series, an autographed photograph of Francine Pascal, plus a SWEET VALLEY HIGH® T-shirt (approximate retail value: $20.00).

3) Enter as often as you wish but each entry must be mailed in a separate envelope bearing sufficient postage. All completed entries must be postmarked and received by Bantam no later than March 15, 1989 in order to be eligible. Entries become the property of Bantam Books and none will be returned. Each description of your favorite prank must be typed or neatly printed on the entry card. The winning pranks will be judged by Bantam's Young Readers Marketing Department on the basis of originality and creativity and all of Bantam's decisions are final and binding. Winners will be notified by mail on or about March 30, 1989. All prizes will be awarded. Winners have 30 days from the date of Bantam's notice in which to claim their prize award or an alternative winner will be chosen. Odds of winning are dependent on the number of entries received. A prize won by a minor will be awarded to a parent or legal guardian. Limit one prize per household or address. No prize substitutions or transfers allowed. Bantam is not responsible for lost or misdirected entries.

4) Prize winners and their parents or legal guardians may be required to execute an Affidavit Of Eligibility And Promotional Release supplied by Bantam. Entering the contest constitutes permission for use of the prize winner's contest submission, name, address and likeness for publicity and promotional purposes, with no additional compensation.

5) Employees of Bantam Books, Bantam/Doubleday/Dell Publishing Group, Inc., their subsidiaries and affiliates, and their immediate family members are not eligible to enter this contest. This contest is open to residents of the U.S. and Canada and is void wherever prohibited or restricted by law. Canadian winners may be required to correctly answer a skill question in order to receive their prize. All applicable federal, state and local regulations apply. Taxes, if any, are the winner's sole responsibility.